"If I can end this right now, I will."

Ivy's entire being ached to race up the once-safe little dirt path to her house. Surely, if she buried her head beneath her pillows, she'd wake up and discover this was a horrific nightmare.

Instead, she dug in her heels. "Let Linc help you. I'll lay on the floorboard of his truck out of sight while—"

"Whoever's in the car could have an accomplice. I'm going after this guy."

"Jacob—" Her voice was desperate, but she didn't care. He couldn't do this.

Jacob stopped and turned her to face him. The commanding expression softened, and his voice dropped low, pleading. "Please. So I know you're safe. Think about Wren."

She wanted to argue, to protect him, but he was right. Her daughter—their daughter—needed to come first.

No matter the cost.

"Run straight to Linc's truck. No looking back. I'll see you as soon as we have this guy in custody and the sheriff takes him." His eyes scanned hers.

He pulled away and turned her toward Linc's truck before jogging away.

Back into danger...

Jodie Bailey writes novels about freedom and the heroes who fight for it. Her novel *Crossfire* won a 2015 RT Reviewers' Choice Best Book Award. She is convinced a camping trip to the beach with her family, a good cup of coffee and a great book can cure all ills. Jodie lives in North Carolina with her husband, her daughter and two dogs.

Books by Jodie Bailey

Love Inspired Suspense

Visit the Author Profile page at LoveInspired.com.

WITNESS IN PERIL

JODIE BAILEY

LOVE INSPIRED SUSPENSE

INSPIRATIONAL ROMANCE

LOVE INSPIRED® SUSPENSE
INSPIRATIONAL ROMANCE

ISBN-13: 978-1-335-55494-9

Recycling programs
for this product may
not exist in your area.

Witness in Peril

This edition published by arrangement with Harlequin Books S.A.

For questions and comments about the quality of this book, please contact us at CustomerService@Harlequin.com.

Love Inspired
22 Adelaide St. West, 41st Floor
Toronto, Ontario M5H 4E3, Canada
www.LoveInspired.com

Printed in U.S.A.

There is no fear in love;
but perfect love casteth out fear: because fear hath
torment. He that feareth is not made perfect in love.
—*1 John* 4:18

To Christina,

So many years on this journey, and we've gotten to walk it together every step of the way.

How awesome is life
when God throws "random" people together?

I'm so glad He knows what He's doing
and that He gave me a friend like you.

ONE

A woman's scream ripped through the small brick house, drowning out the echo of the doorbell Ivy Bridges had just pressed.

Gripping the folder that contained a legal form needing Clarissa Mendez's signature, Ivy took one step backward on the front stoop of the small brick house on Ashton Road. The heel of her ankle boot slipped on the edge of the step, and she reached for the wooden railing. Surely that scream hadn't come from inside. Surely she'd heard—

Another scream, this one choked off in the middle as though an invisible hand squeezed the sound into submission.

Clarissa Mendez was in trouble.

Ivy glanced at her car, ready to run for safety, but she couldn't. Clarissa clearly needed help, and if Ivy bolted while it was in her power to help, she'd never be able to forgive herself.

Dropping the folder, she reached into her purse and dug for her pepper spray. She'd learned the hard way a couple of years ago that a female lawyer could never be too careful, even one who only handled estates, business law and family issues.

But this moment felt far more dangerous than when Harlan Whittaker had screamed at her on Main Street for refusing to represent him in his bid to be named executor of his real-estate-millionaire uncle's estate.

This sounded like the kind of danger that required the police.

From past experience, she already knew her cell got zero reception on the Mendez property, which was nearly ten miles outside the small town of Swift River, Utah, near the Nevada/Arizona/Utah border. If anyone was going to help Clarissa, it had to be Ivy.

She squared her shoulders. *Please, Lord, let her have seen a really big spider.* Spiders she could handle. Anything worse…

Shuddering, Ivy peeked into the window beside the door, but gauzy sheer curtains covered the panes, revealing nothing inside. With a prayer for protection, she reached for the doorknob.

The door was already ajar. Hopefully, if this was simply a spider situation, Clarissa would understand why Ivy had invaded her privacy.

Flicking the "safety" on the pepper spray, Ivy eased into the entryway, scanning the small living room where Clarissa's uncle, Edward Mendez, had often parked himself in his recliner to watch black-and-white reruns.

The entire house seemed to be holding its breath. No sound drifted to her. Even the birds outside were silent. There was no way she'd imagined those screams, was there?

Ivy cleared her throat and stepped deeper into the house, heading for the swinging door that led to the kitchen. "Clarissa?" Her voice rasped, a result of the adrenaline from her pounding heart.

No one answered.

Shoving open the swinging door, Ivy peeked into the kitchen, then slipped inside, keeping her boot heels light on the old yellow linoleum floor.

Ivy glanced around the room, her chest tightening. Two chairs at the kitchen table were overturned. Cooked rice clung to a cabinet door and dripped from the countertop onto the floor.

Every thought screamed at Ivy to run, but she couldn't, not if Clarissa needed her.

A cooking pot lay on its side near the half-open accordion doors that led to the laundry room on the far side of the kitchen.

Cold fear ran along Ivy's skin. This was more than a spider sighting. Something was very wrong. She should leave, drive up the road until she got a signal and call the police. But what if she was overreacting?

It didn't feel like overreacting. It felt more as though eyes watched her from every direction.

"Clarissa?" This time she whispered, her gut twisting, telling her there were answers behind the half-open door to the laundry room.

Gently, Ivy slid open the door. A bare foot came into view, then a blue-jean-clad leg. Clarissa Mendez lay motionless on the floor by the dryer. Her blank eyes stared unseeing at the ceiling. From the angle of her head, it was clear that nothing could be done to revive the woman.

A scream clogged Ivy's throat. Her stomach threatened to revolt. Her breathing came in puffs, but there was not enough air. Not nearly enough. Her feet retreated of their own will. *No. No. No.* She was not seeing this.

Ivy turned to run, to get out, to find help.

She collided with a human wall. The pepper spray flew from her hand and bounced off the wall. Her purse slid from her shoulder and hit the floor by her feet with a thud.

Strong hands gripped her elbows, squeezing tightly, holding her at arm's length.

A man with an angular chin and blond hair surveyed her, his jaw set. He wore a suit, and a silver-star badge hung on a cord around his neck.

A US Marshal.

Ivy nearly slumped in relief. "Deputy. How did you get here so—"

He shook her, and her head jerked. His eyes hardened with rage.

The breath caught in Ivy's throat. This was not her salvation.

This was her undoing.

A scream expanded in her lungs, pushing outward, drawing pain but refusing release. A whimper escaped instead.

The man pulled her through the door then drove her backward against the kitchen wall.

Pain jolted through her shoulder blade on impact.

He pinned her, standing so close she couldn't move. Scanning her face, he sneered, "If it isn't Ivy Bridges."

How did he know her name? Ivy struggled, but he'd leaned all of his weight into his hands, holding her fast to the wall.

"You've saved me a trip to your office. Or to your house."

Her house? Ivy fought harder. If he knew about her house, he knew she had a daughter.

He could *not* get to her daughter.

Pressing his forearm against her chest, the man wrapped his gloved hand around her neck and squeezed. "Too bad you've seen me, maybe even seen my partner. Guess I'll check your car for your files or head to your office and grab them for myself." He squeezed tighter. "Or are they at your house? Does your daughter know where Mommy keeps her work papers?"

Ivy gagged and fought for air, her trachea aching and burning against the pressure. Dark spots danced before her eyes. Blood pounded in her head and neck.

Her daughter. She had to protect her daughter.

With the last of her waning strength, she drove her knee upward, praying it would make contact.

The man howled and stumbled away, but only slightly.

It was enough.

Ivy ducked sideways and ran for the door.

He dove for her, smashing into the table and shoving it into the drywall on the other side of the kitchen.

The pent-up scream finally exploded into the air. Ivy ran for the front door as the man roared her name.

She burst onto the porch, then jumped the steps and landed hard on the grass. She was desperate to reach Wren. To get to the corner of Murphy and Deer Path Roads, where she should pick up a cell signal.

She had to get to her SUV before that man got to her. And she practically screamed a prayer of thanks that her key fob was in her jeans pocket and not in her purse.

Her purse... Which was on the floor in the laundry room.

The front door banged open as Ivy reached her SUV. She threw herself into the vehicle and started the engine.

The man raced toward her, colliding with the door as

she started the car. He struck the window with the side of his fist, murder in his expression. With one last glance at her assailant, Ivy shifted the car into Reverse and roared backward out of the dirt driveway.

From the yard, he screamed at her, then turned and ran toward the bend in the road, likely where he'd parked his car.

Ivy shifted to Drive and floored it, throwing dirt and gravel from the unpaved road. All she had to do was get to the main road, to civilization.

To get a call to the police and an officer to Wren's preschool. How had that man known about her daughter?

And why was he wearing a US Marshals badge? One that he clearly didn't mind being seen?

Her hands trembled on the wheel, and she fought to control the car at the speed she was traveling. Her life was in danger. And Clarissa Mendez was dead.

Who would want to hurt Clarissa? She was friendly and helpful—everyone in Swift River adored Clarissa.

Now in her midforties, Clarissa had moved to town as a teenager, after her parents were killed in a car accident in Massachusetts. She'd lived with her uncle, a widower who owned Moments in Time, an antiques store on historic Main Street. Edward Mendez had passed away of complications from heart surgery just a few weeks ago. Clarissa was executor of the will and now the sole proprietor of the store. Ivy was helping settle the estate.

But Clarissa was dead. Killed by a man with the uniform, badge and bearing of a federal law-enforcement officer.

Ivy nearly lost the back end of the car making the turn onto Deer Path Road. *Finally.* Pavement instead of dirt. Her heart pounded a rhythm with the thoughts in her head. *A few more minutes*. She glanced at the radio display, where the link to her phone indicated one bar.

Ivy pressed the emergency call button, but the signal dropped immediately. Not enough.

Gritting her teeth, she glanced in the rearview mirror.

A car whipped out of a side road and came up fast. *No*. She pressed harder on the accelerator, the tires humming on the asphalt as the car behind her drew closer.

Blue lights suddenly flashed in her rearview.

Her breath left her lungs in a rush. The car bore the blue-and-black markings of the Swift River Police Department.

She lifted her foot from the accelerator and almost sagged in the seat. For the first time in her life, she was grateful for a speed trap.

Gliding to a stop, Ivy rolled down her window and placed her shaking hands at ten and two on the steering wheel, watching the officer.

He stepped out of the car awfully fast. He hadn't even taken the time to call in her plate. Or slap a hat on over his rumpled brown hair. Driving ninety on a back road was probably a more urgent offense than going sixty in a forty-five, but still, she hadn't done anything to put him into such a rush.

Something in her stomach writhed with a sickening twist. This didn't feel right. A thought tugged at her, and she tightened her hands on the steering wheel. She was still in the county, but not inside the town limits. This wasn't the police department's jurisdiction. No Swift River officer would be stopping speeders here.

No Swift River officer would look as disheveled as this one did.

As the officer stepped closer, he raised his hands and trained his pistol on her vehicle. It looked like a revolver.

The local police officers carried department-issued semiautomatics. She'd seen them often around the courthouse.

The growl from the man at the Mendez house echoed in her head. *Too bad you've seen me, maybe even seen my partner.*

Without considering the consequences if she was wrong, Ivy shifted into gear and floored it, throwing road rubble onto the officer. There was a *thwack* as a bullet hit the liftgate of her SUV. Another hit seconds later.

Terrified, Ivy whimpered as tears clogged her throat. She had no idea what she'd stumbled into. She only knew she had to run, that she and Wren were both in danger.

And she couldn't trust the police.

There was only one person in law enforcement she could trust, but he was two hours away.

And he might turn her away when he found out she was carrying a secret that would change his life forever.

Thunder cracked and rain poured off the metal roof. The small amount of shelter did nothing to protect Jacob Garcia's front stoop from the lashing of a March storm near the Grand Canyon. The torrent dripped off the roof, straight beneath his collar and down his back as he fumbled the keys.

Someday, he'd find a way to tack a bigger porch onto the old family cabin. Better yet, he'd build a garage.

Check that thought. His sister would never allow a garage. It wouldn't match the plan Angie, a meteorologist with the National Weather Service, had created with several conservation groups. They were converting the private ranch into an area for scientific research and for artist retreats, restoring the land and creating a place where art and research came together to preserve and appreciate the canyon's natural beauty.

Stepping into the log house, Jacob shut the door on the driving storm. *Finally.* He slipped off his hat and hung it on a peg by the front door, scrubbing his hand across his short, dark, drenched hair. After shuddering out of his windbreaker, he hung the coat to drip-dry over the slate tiles so it wouldn't puddle on the hardwood floor he'd refinished only a month earlier.

Nestled inside a grove of spruce and fir trees not far from the Kaibab National Forest on the canyon's south rim, the original log cabin had been built in the 1850s by his great-many-times-over-grandfather and added on to over the years, until the newer ranch house was constructed. The "new" house sat a winding back-road mile from where he now stood, about seven miles from the rim.

A soft sound from the back of the cabin, near the bedrooms, stopped him before he could sit down on the bench and remove his muddy boots. Hand on his service weapon, he cocked his head and listened, trying to hear past the lashing wind and rain.

Either something had blown against the house or he was more exhausted than he'd first thought. He'd been out in the elements for too long, investigating a death on the north rim of the nearby Grand Canyon. His team, part of a National Park Service special investigation unit that tracked violent criminals and antiquities smugglers in and around the canyon, had taken point on the case. The dead man bore a striking resemblance to a suspect they'd been tracking for months, but it had ultimately proven to be a case of mistaken identity.

Witness statements and identification indicated the man who had tumbled over the edge was a lone hiker who'd ventured too close to the rim. The tragedy warranted no further investigation, but it still carried the weight of death, of a family somewhere who'd lost a loved one too soon.

The smuggler, Daniel Adams, was alive and well, it seemed.

Dropping onto the bench by the door, he shucked off his boots and ran through tomorrow's agenda. His day off was intact since the case no longer involved their special investigative unit.

He headed across the den, where his leather recliner waited for him at an angle to the red plaid sofa that was a hand-me-down from Angie. At least the huge flat-screen over the old river-stone fireplace was his own purchase. Three years with the military police, then another two training and working toward this position, hadn't left him a whole lot of time to collect his own personal home furnishings, but that was all changing now that he finally had the chance to settle down into life as an investigator and a confirmed bachelor.

Not that it had been his choice to get out of the army so soon. The increasing pain in his lower back reminded him he'd worked too hard today and would likely pay the price tomorrow with a nice little visit from the injury that had sidelined his plans to be a lifer in service to the United States.

Hooah.

No use thinking about what he couldn't get back. And no use dwelling on what an IED on a mountain path in

Afghanistan had stolen from him. He couldn't rewind time and fix any of it.

But wouldn't it be nice if he could? He'd repair a lot more than his busted body, that was for sure.

As he passed between the couch and the recliner, he bent forward to turn on the lamp that rested on the end table, but his fingers froze on the switch. Peeking from beneath the edge of the natural wood table was a pair of muddy brown boots.

Boots that were not his.

Straightening, Jacob glanced around his living room, listening. Tightening his fingers around the grip of his pistol, he eased it from the holster and held it low in both hands. The open living room, kitchen and dining room revealed no other signs of an intruder. Whoever it was had to be up the short hallway, either in his bedroom or in the spare room, which he kept closed off to make it easier to heat the house with the log fireplace.

Jacob crept slowly to the head of the hallway, avoiding the floorboards that always creaked. He pressed his back against the wall, out of the line of fire if someone decided to charge at him with guns blazing. "Federal agent! Come out now with your hands where I can see them!"

The echo of his authority died into silence, but then a door creaked open. The spare room.

He gripped the gun tighter and prepared to peek around the corner. "Hands away from your body where I can see them."

"They are. I'm not armed." The voice belonged to a female. "It's me, Jacob."

His head jerked back. The voice was not only feminine, but it was also familiar. Surely he was imagining things. There was no way she was in his house.

Steeling himself against the sight of her and fully pre-pared to discover his mind was playing tricks on him, Jacob leaned slightly around the corner, his senses on high alert.

In the dim light from the lamp behind him, a woman stood in the guest-room doorway, her hands above her head, her dark hair waving to her shoulders. Her brown-eyed gaze was uncertain and wavering.

His heart pounded and his fingers nearly lost their grip on the pistol as he tried to holster it.

Ivy Bridges.

The woman he'd left behind five years before.

TWO

"Jacob?" Ivy's hands trembled above her head. Actually looking him in the eye on the heels of the afternoon's attacks might be the thing that finally took her down. The last time she'd seen him—

Ivy's eyes slipped shut. The last time she'd seen him had changed both of their lives, although only one of them knew it.

"You can put your hands down." He eyed her warily as he slipped the pistol into a holster at his hip. "Ivy." The way he said her name, it was almost as though he doubted she was actually in front of him. "What are you doing here?"

Lowering her hands, Ivy reached behind her and pulled the bedroom door shut. Wren had fallen asleep only a few minutes before, and Ivy wasn't ready for her to wake up. Wasn't ready to see her with Jacob. That time would come soon enough. There was too much more to deal with first.

Like murder. And threats. And two men who should have tried to protect her trying to kill her instead.

Now that she was reasonably safe, her mind spun

with the ways she could have died. Her hand went to her throat, where she could still feel gloved fingers.

Ivy opened her mouth, but a violent tremor silenced her. She'd been holding back emotions since she buckled Wren in the car, then pressed the gas pedal to make the long drive to the only law-enforcement officer she was certain she could trust. Her hands shook. Her insides shook. Everything shook.

Ivy wrapped her arms around her waist and eyed the man who used to be her entire world. Until the day he'd signed away their future, choosing a path in life that they'd never discussed and she could never follow.

Something in his posture relaxed, and he exhaled loudly. "You're soaking wet. Do you have dry clothes?"

She didn't. Ivy had raced to the church to get Wren from day care, afraid to ask for help, not knowing whom she could trust. She'd called 911 to report Clarissa's murder, dumped her cell phone in a trash can at the church and fled for Arizona, praying she'd evaded those men.

"Okay." Jacob dragged his hand down his cheek. "If you'll go back into the spare room, Angie left some clothes in the dresser when she moved to the main house."

"Thank you." The words came out on a whisper. She wanted to say more, but nothing would come. Maybe it was the trauma. Or maybe her head was afraid that her mouth would pour out confessions neither of them were ready for.

Ivy slipped into the bedroom, still shivering. The room held a full-size bed and a small dresser. The wood floor was cold beneath her feet. She'd just shucked off her shoes and socks when Jacob had stomped up to the front door and she'd ducked into hiding, terrified she'd been followed.

Several shirts, some leggings and a few pairs of jeans were in the dresser. Once she was warm and dry in an oversize Grand Canyon sweatshirt, leggings and thick boot socks, Ivy felt more human, more capable and less like a quivering mass of gelatin.

She leaned over the bed to check on Wren. Her daughter was curled on her side, one fist buried beneath her cheek. Her dark hair flowed over the pillow in damp tangles. Wren was a champion sleeper, able to snooze through anything from car horns to thunderstorms.

Ivy pressed a light kiss to her slumbering daughter's forehead. For the moment, they were safe.

But she was about to walk out that door and make a confession Jacob would never see coming. And after she'd rocked his life, she was going to dare to ask for his help. Burying her face in her hands, she wished she'd had anywhere else to run. This was unfair to Jacob, and it was killing her heart all over again.

After shaking out her hands, Ivy slipped into the hallway and shut the door, then walked carefully across the hardwood, the creaking floor accusing her with every step.

Jacob was in the kitchen with his back to her, heating water on the stove. He'd changed into track pants and a gray sweatshirt. While the breadth of his back and shoulders indicated he still had muscle, he was leaner than he'd been in college, likely the result of the injury that had ended his military career and brought him back to Arizona. Mutual friends had kept her in the loop. She'd wanted to reach out to him but the secret she carried stopped her.

She sat on a stool at the bar, lacing her fingers in her lap. What did a girl say to the guy who'd left her behind?

To the man who was the father of her child? A child he didn't even know existed?

He looked over his shoulder. "Tea?"

She nodded and found her voice. Tea was safe. She could talk about tea. "You gave up coffee?" He'd been a hard-core coffee guzzler all through college and law school. When some turned to alcohol and worse, Jacob embraced brew from beans.

"I gave up caffeine after—" He tipped his head toward the ceiling, then pulled a box from the cabinet, dropped tea bags into two mugs and poured water over them. He crossed the kitchen and approached her, then slid a mug across the polished wood bar. "I gave up caffeine a couple of years ago, but like a smoker needs something to do with their hands, I needed something to carry in a travel mug."

Wrapping her hands around the thick blue mug, Ivy let the warmth run up her arms and into the ice that had lodged in her heart. "I'm sorry I surprised you. I assumed you lived in the main house with your sister. I was going to find you in the morning. It was a shock to see the place fixed up. I should have left, but..." But where else would she go?

"About that." Shoving his mug aside, Jacob leaned his forearms on the counter. "How'd you get in?"

Ivy swirled the red-tinted brew in her mug. It smelled like cherries and tasted like summer. "I remembered the window off the laundry room didn't lock." In college, when she'd visited his family on breaks, they'd sneaked into the old cabin and dreamed what it would be like to fix it up someday. "It looks different." Almost like they'd once imagined as they sat on the dusty floor near where the stove now rested, his arm around her and her head on his shoulder, their future bright and shiny.

Two weeks before they graduated law school, when she'd expected an engagement ring, he'd flipped the script and signed over his life to his country. It was a life Ivy couldn't live, one that had already stolen so much from her. There were still nights when she lay awake, unable to shake the image of men in army dress uniform on their doorstep, bringing news of her father's death during a Joint Task Force North mission on the border with Mexico.

"We might use the cabin as a guest house someday." Jacob's dark eyes pinned hers, and it was like falling into a time machine. He was likely reliving the same memories that were swirling in her head. Past, present and the ashes of a once-dreamed future all whirled in her mental tornado. "Ivy, you know what question I'm not asking."

Why are you here? He'd asked earlier, and she owed him an answer. Still, it took several seconds for the words to form. Saying them out loud made the horror even more real. "Someone tried to kill me."

"What?" Backing away from the counter, Jacob dragged a hand through his thick dark hair. "Are you…?" He rounded the bar and sat on the stool beside hers. "Tell me everything."

Ivy told her story, but she did so without looking him in the eye. If she saw concern, it would undo her. "I didn't know where else to go, not when they both seemed to be law enforcement."

Jacob tapped the counter, and he scanned the kitchen as though he could read a plan in the air. "Why would he ask for your files? Is there anything out of the ordinary about the estate you're settling for the victim?" He stopped tapping and looked directly at her. "Has anything strange happened prior to this?"

She'd gone over the estate in her head for most of the two-hour drive. "It's a straightforward estate. Mr. Mendez passed away and left everything to Clarissa. She was already a partner in his antiques store. Clarissa had just brought me some hard copies of stocks and bonds. Those are mostly electronic now, so it's unusual to have the actual papers. I haven't had a chance to look through them, but it's possible they're worth something. I can't speak for Clarissa and strange happenings. I knew her, but not well. As for me—"

Wait. Ivy's jaw slackened as unrelated incidents began to come together. "It could be nothing, but the past week or so there have been…things."

"Like?"

"Twice I thought a car followed me when I left the office at the end of the day, but I figured it was just the typical *noticing* I do." Reading too many suspense novels sometimes made her paranoid. "My admin assistant, Kendra, thought the door lock at the office was acting up. She wondered if someone had tried to pick it, but I dismissed it." Kendra was a fan of true-crime podcasts, particularly Christi Cold's *Dead Talk*. "I thought she was imagining things."

"Where's your office?"

"The second floor of the old Swift River Savings and Loan building, downtown."

The tapping on the counter started again. It was an old habit that revealed his agitation. "If those two were a federal cop and a local police officer, then we'll keep my name out of this so no one looks for you here. You'll have to lay low here until we can figure out what happens next."

"Thank you. I just want this to be over. They threatened me. Threatened Wren."

"Wren?" Jacob grabbed his mug, then slid off his stool and walked to the sink. "Who's Wren?"

Ivy balled her fists in her lap. Of all the ways she'd imagined telling him the truth, this one wasn't even on the list. Given the shocking amount of information she'd unloaded on him already, now wasn't the best time to add that Wren was his daughter, but he'd know as soon as he saw her.

When they'd parted ways after graduation, her heart had been in shards that never truly healed. She'd promised herself in that moment that she'd let him go and not try to drag him away from what he had determined to be right. Had promised herself she'd never marry a man who could be gone in an instant, ripped from the very country he sought to protect. She wouldn't put her future children through the pain that she had been through when her father was killed. She'd craved safety, security, a stable home, not constant moving and a husband who could be gone in an instant, either to the "needs of the army" or to the kind of death that only came in nightmares.

She'd kept that promise when Wren was born. The space for "father's name" on her birth certificate was blank.

Something in Jacob's gut twisted. Maybe he shouldn't have guzzled herbal tea before starting this conversation. Ivy was in danger. Someone—possibly law-enforcement officers—had tried to kill her.

Twice.

But the look on her face now hinted that there was something more.

This wasn't fear. The way she shifted her gaze to her hands in her lap suggested something else… Guilt.

And who was Wren?

"What are you not telling me?" He leaned his hip against the counter by the sink, keeping distance between them. If she'd committed a crime, he couldn't get involved. He'd have to stay true to his duty and the oaths he'd taken.

But when tears hovered in the corners of her eyes and threatened to spill over, it was all he could do not to cast it aside while promising to do whatever it took to keep her safe.

Her mouth opened then closed again. Finally, she pressed her fingers to her eyes, squared her shoulders as if she'd made a decision and stood. Without looking back, she walked toward the hall, motioning for him to follow.

At the door to the spare room, she stopped with her hand on the iron doorknob and her head bowed toward the heavy wooden planks. Shaking her head, she opened the door and stepped aside, staring at her feet. "I'm sorry."

The words were a whisper he barely heard. They landed somewhere in his chest with a chill he wasn't certain how to interpret. Careful not to touch her as he passed, he slipped into the room.

In the reflected light from the hallway, a little girl slept peacefully, her hand tucked under her cheek and her dark hair fanning over the pillow. Ivy had a daughter?

He looked at Ivy, his eyebrows knitting together in silent question, but she was watching the child.

He stepped closer to the bed, questions swirling with each step. Why hadn't she said something earlier? Was

Ivy married? The little girl looked to be about the same age as his cousin's daughter, maybe three or four years old, so—

His heart almost stopped beating. Even the sound of the rain on the roof seemed to retreat. *Three or four years.* Four years plus nine months…

In a couple of months, it would be five years since he and Ivy had parted.

I'm sorry. Suddenly her words made sense. They slammed him in the back, urging him closer to the little girl. The little girl with the nose he recognized from his own baby pictures.

His little girl.

His breath stuttered and stopped. *His little girl.*

Words and emotions struggled inside him, the fight almost physical. This was too much. Too heavy. Too… He spun on his heel toward Ivy, who wouldn't meet his eye, then stared at the little girl again.

Wren. Ivy had called her Wren.

Jacob shook his head, then shoved past Ivy. He couldn't look at her. Why hadn't she told him?

He stalked up the hallway and out the front door.

Cold rain blasted skin that burned from the inside out. There should have been steam rising off him. He was a mixture of adrenaline and outrage and shock. He had no idea where he was going until he almost stumbled against the restored '76 Ford his father had once driven on the ranch and Jacob now drove daily.

The door squeaked in protest as he hauled it open. He climbed inside, then slammed the door and held on to the steering wheel with both hands, as though it would keep him from flying off the planet, fueled by his out-of-control emotions.

He was a father. Ivy was a mother. They had a little girl. Together.

All the air left his lungs in a heated rush. The weight of truth bowed him until his forehead rested on the steering wheel, his fists against his cheeks.

The rain pounding the roof began to ease, but the quieting roar only made Ivy's voice louder in his head.

They threatened me. Threatened Wren.

He had a daughter, and she was in danger.

"Oh, God…" The plea ripped out on jagged edges that tore the back of his throat. "God…" He was a child, crying out for his Father. Weak. Whimpering. *Explain this, God. Make it make sense. Make it not hurt.*

Because it did hurt. With the same kind of ripping, tearing pain that had assaulted him when an IED exploded on a winter afternoon in Afghanistan.

But this time the roar in his ears came from inside. The pain pressed outward against his ribs from his heart. Something wanted to claw its way to the surface, but he had no idea what.

He'd survived that day, but he might not now.

He had a daughter. Him. The shattered soldier who'd been told two years ago that he'd never hold a child of his own. A daughter who'd come into the world with a cry, who'd said her first words and taken her first steps without him.

God, it hurts.

The rain eased into nothing, leaving an eerie silence in its wake. He let his head drop farther, as he maintained his death grip on the steering wheel. He'd missed it. All of it. From the first heartbeat to the bedtime story Ivy had probably told before she tucked their daughter in on this very night. All of it.

And Ivy…

Ivy had kept his daughter away from him.

He jerked suddenly, arching his back, throwing his face toward the sky. What he wanted was to scream until his throat was raw, but the sound stuck in his throat. He ached to start the truck and drive until this made sense.

He needed to talk to his sister, at the very least. But his keys and phone were in the house.

He let out a bitter laugh. Inside the house was a daughter he didn't know. A woman who'd betrayed him.

And somewhere out there were two men who wanted them dead.

Dipping his chin, he stared out the windshield toward the canyon. The trees around the house faded into the pitch-dark, where anything or anyone could hide.

With a daughter to protect, that darkness hid more dangers than he'd ever considered before.

"Why, God?" Supposedly, God was closer than the air in this truck. If that was true, He clearly wasn't very fond of Jacob Garcia. "I gave up Ivy to be a soldier. I bent my whole life to that, turned my back on a law career to follow what You asked of me. I gave everything up, Lord. All of it. And then not even three years in, Your calling got blasted away. And I don't know who I am. I don't know what You want me to be or do. But apparently…" He laughed again, a strange mixture of bitter anger and honeyed joy. "Apparently You want me to be a dad."

He leaned forward and pressed his cold fingers to his hot forehead.

Tears hardened in his throat. He wouldn't cry.

But he was a dad.

Right now, he could walk into that house, pick up his daughter and rock her in the recliner until his heart settled into understanding and contentment. Until his insides quieted. And what could Ivy do to prevent that?

Nothing. Because he was Wren's father.

Only Wren wouldn't have a clue who he was.

Even as his heart warmed toward his daughter, it wasn't enough to make him feel anything but cold anger toward Ivy. *Daughter... Betrayed...* The words were at war.

How could she not tell him? And now she'd only confessed because she needed someone to protect her.

And Wren.

A timid knock lifted his head. He turned to the sound and found Ivy standing by the passenger side of the truck, her expression heavy.

He looked away, out the driver's side. After the raging storm and the bone-rattling earthquake of Ivy's news, his emotions collapsed. It was the same feeling he'd had after each panic attack that had shaken him as he fought through his physical recovery at Brooke Army Medical Center. He felt the same as he had then, like he was standing outside of himself, viewing someone else's life. Some poor sap who'd just found out the woman he used to love—the one who still haunted his dreams—had kept the world's most precious gift from him.

Ivy apparently didn't read the room well, because she slid into the truck, shutting the door as she laid his jacket on his lap. "You left in the rain."

Her statement made him realize just how chilled he was in his soaking-wet clothes. Although he was about to start shivering until his teeth chattered, there was no way he'd give her the satisfaction of putting that coat on. She didn't get to start doing nice things for him now, not after keeping his daughter a secret. "How old is she?"

"She turned four on February seventeenth."

"What's her full name?"

Ivy sniffed, staring at her knee.

"Ivy?"

Her indrawn breath shook. "Wren Antónia Bridges."

Antónia. After him. His middle name. Antonio.

He turned, wanting to see her face. Needing to know the words she spoke were truth. "Why not tell me?"

This time, she looked him straight in the eye. "You left."

"This is not my fault."

"It's not." She shook her head. "But we planned a life together. For over five years, we talked about the future. I expected an engagement, not an enlistment."

It was his turn to look away. He'd blindsided her. Had blindsided himself really. In the wake of his father's death, he'd felt so lost until a chance conversation with an army recruiter had filled him with a sense of purpose again. He'd signed without discussing it with Ivy, afraid she'd talk him out of it. Instead of confessing he was lost, Jacob had claimed to feel called.

He knew how she felt about the military, that she'd hated the constant moving. That she wanted stability. That she still blamed the army for her father's death at the hands of drug smugglers on the Mexican border. "Something in me hoped…" *That you loved me enough to forget your fear.*

"Something in me hoped, too. But if you'd turned away from what you believed was right, you'd have eventually hated me. And if I'd followed, I'd have resented you. You didn't even go in as an officer and a lawyer. You chose the enlisted route. The front line. Dad's death gutted me, but it destroyed Mom. Then I found out you were back, but your job... I couldn't risk Wren being hurt."

"That's not your choice. She's my daughter, too." Saying it out loud almost burst the dam holding his pain.

"Yes. But if I'd called you the month after you left and said, 'Hey, Jakey...'" The way she whined a nickname she'd never once called him was so incongruent with the situation, it almost made him smile. "'Yeah, um, so I'm having your baby.' What would you have thought?"

That maybe we had a future after all. He'd like to imagine that was true. But given the way they'd parted, something in him might have thought she was trying to force him to come back to her. "I don't know."

"When you left, I swore I wouldn't beg you to stay for me. Wren didn't change anything."

"You were wrong." Could she not see that? Had fear so deadened her to others that she lived in a selfishness he'd never noticed?

"I know. But from the moment I first held her, I wanted to shield her. To not force her to live in the pain I'd lived in for so long. It was wrong. And I can never make it right. I can't return what I stole from you. I'm sorry."

Her face tight, she slipped out of the truck and walked back to the house.

Leaving him alone.

THREE

"**W**ell, this doesn't look the greatest." Special Agent Lincoln Tucker's voice was gravelly over the phone with the depth that came from early mornings after late nights. "For starters, Ivy is telling the truth about the murder."

Jacob stared out the window over the kitchen sink at the growing daylight. On the other side of the trees, less than a mile away, the land dropped off into the Grand Canyon. At the gravity in Linc's voice, Jacob's stomach felt as though it had just plummeted over the rim. Part of him had wondered, given Ivy's silence about his daughter, if she was telling the truth about why she'd run. "What are your thoughts?"

He respected Linc's opinion. They'd served together in Afghanistan. It was Linc who'd shown up at the ranch while Jacob was recovering from the concussion of an IED blast that had practically scrambled his insides. His belief that Jacob could regain the strength needed to pass the physical tests for this job with the National Park Service special investigative unit had been enough to spur Jacob back to life. Linc was a solid guy who would use discretion when it came to protecting Ivy…and their daughter.

The daughter who was sound asleep in his spare room. The one he had yet to meet. How did that work? How did a guy say to a kid, "Hey, I'm a stranger, but I'm also your dad?"

Truth be told, he'd spent most of the night forcing himself not to march into that room and introduce himself exactly that way.

Even he knew better than to startle a sleeping child. A child he still couldn't believe was real.

"This is all me doing a quick public search." Linc was still talking, pulling Jacob out of his whirling thoughts. "If the man who murdered Clarissa Mendez was a federal marshal, then he could have files about her flagged, which would lead them straight to me and then to you if I dared to search them. Still, everything your Ivy is saying lines up."

"She's not *my* Ivy." Jacob kept his voice low. The cabin was small, and he didn't need her to overhear. He also didn't need Linc making assumptions, especially not now.

"Whatever you say, dude. But all I heard you talk about overseas was—"

"So what doesn't look good? You led with that." They weren't going down roads best left untraveled, not while he was still reeling from everything that had happened. He'd wrestled most of the night with his feelings, drifting between the shock of seeing Ivy and the anger at her betrayal and the duty of protecting her life and Wren's.

He'd finally landed on that last one. For the moment, he needed to treat this like an investigation. He knew who he was at work, knew what to do. When it came to every other aspect of his life, including Ivy and Wren, there was no playbook.

Linc chuckled, but quickly grew serious. "Ivy's not

a person of interest or a suspect, but her name's floating around, likely because she was a witness and she's technically missing. Her purse was found at the scene."

"She's also a victim." The last thing they needed was a bad actor casting suspicion on her. If someone framed her, there would be little he could do. He'd have to see that she turned herself in. That was his duty.

"Nobody is suggesting she's guilty, but given that local law enforcement likely has questions…"

"The sheriff's department will probably want a statement in person." It was the exact thing he'd been afraid of from the moment she'd told her story. But taking her back to Swift River could prove deadly.

"At the very least, they need to know she's safe so they don't open a missing-person case."

That was true as well. There was no reason to let the Dow County sheriff waste resources, especially not now.

"Garcia, if you were a civilian, I'd say wait until they issued some sort of warrant. But as a law-enforcement officer? Ethics and professional courtesy kick in." Something over the phone rustled. Knowing Linc, he was shifting the device from one ear to the other, as he often did. "My suggestion? Escort her to Swift River. I can tag along, make sure you don't pick up a tail and keep an eye on your back."

"Given that one of her assailants was driving a Swift River PD cruiser, we might be okay talking to the sheriff. It's two different agencies in two different towns." He'd checked. The main sheriff's office was in the county seat, not in Swift River.

"Marginally safer, but I agree."

Jacob scrubbed his palm down his cheek, scratching against a day's worth of stubble. Outside the window over the sink, the world was pink and orange, the proof that morning really could come after the darkest night. Yeah, his night had been long. Ivy had walked back into his life and dropped half a decade's worth of bombs in one pass.

He needed to deal with them one at a time. "I'll call you after I talk to Ivy, but my guess is we're on the move today, if you really do want to follow." They set up a tentative schedule for the two-hour drive, then Jacob killed the call and settled his phone onto the plank wood counter.

Are You doing something here, God? And how am I supposed to handle this? He'd grown up praying, believing God was in charge of his life, but he'd struggled after the IED destroyed the calling he'd given up Ivy and a law career to follow. In the past few months, though, he'd found himself drawing near again, trying to figure out who God wanted him to be in this new normal. Trying to find peace.

Too bad he couldn't seem to feel a whole lot of that peace at the moment. He wanted to see Wren. Wanted to hug her. To look her in the eye and see if he could find the half of her DNA that was his. She had his nose and hair. What about her eyes? Was her smile his? Or was it Ivy's? Those long lashes that had brushed her cheeks in her sleep were definitely Ivy's.

Ivy's lashes. His nose. A tiny human being existed, one who had seemingly been made up of the best parts of them both. Their once-shared dreams of a life together existed in their…daughter.

It didn't seem possible. The ache of it was both sweet and bitter. He had a daughter, but he'd missed her fluttery baby kicks and her birth. Her first word and her first steps.

The loss iced his heart, colder than the rain he'd shivered in the night before, chilling any warm emotions he might have toward the woman he'd once thought he'd always love, if only as a tender memory.

"Hey."

The creaking floor, along with her greeting, announced Ivy's approach.

Bent on saying the words that had pressed against his chest the entire night, that were begging to be unleashed on her, he turned.

She stood at the end of the bar, Wren in her arms, the little girl's face buried in her neck. The redness of Ivy's eyes and the dark circles beneath them spoke of a sleepless night and probably tears as well.

The angry words Jacob had wanted to hurl at her flamed hot, then crumbled into ashes. Their daughter did not need to be burned by his hurt and anger. And Ivy didn't need more guilt heaped on her when she was clearly in pain.

But what about his pain? Four years ago, in February, what had he been doing at the moment this life came into the world? When she was drawing her first breath?

He'd been living his life for himself. Oblivious.

The dark, heated words seared his throat again, but he swallowed them. They could come later. This moment was about something entirely different.

It was about meeting his daughter.

Instinctively, he stepped to the two of them but stopped less than an arm's length away, his hand outstretched toward his daughter's back. His gaze went to Ivy's. Could he…?

She was watching him, her expression unreadable, but she nodded.

How was it he had to have permission to address his own daughter? Somehow, he felt like he'd done something wrong, like he had to earn his own flesh and blood's love and trust.

Biting down on that ire one more time, he set it aside to dwell on later. Right now, he didn't want anything negative to bruise this moment.

Gently, he rested his hand on her back, shifting closer to Ivy. In another lifetime, this could have been their normal, everyday life. From the outside, it probably looked like a perfect picture.

It was an illusion.

Wren was sleep-warmed, and her back shifted slightly beneath his palm each time she breathed. She was alive and real. She had a beating heart and a thinking brain. She was probably the smartest four-year-old in the world.

And she was his. This adorable, precious life was his child. "Hi, Wren. I'm—" He sniffed and kept his gaze fixed on the back of Wren's tangled dark hair, refusing to look at Ivy for a cue. This was his child. He'd introduce himself his way.

No. He'd introduce himself in the way that was best for Wren. "I'm Jacob."

Arching her back in a lazy stretch, Wren turned her head and eyed him with a sleepy expression. Something about her sparked and twinkled with mischief. After a moment, she yawned. "I Wren." She lifted her head and patted Ivy's neck. "This is Mama."

He wanted to tap his palm against his chest, where his heart had been before she snatched it out of him. *This is Daddy.* Tears of wonder and joy and sadness stung his nose. Digging his teeth into the inside of his lower lip, he capped that well. That kind of emotion from him would disturb Wren. "I'm sure you have a very good mama."

Wren's nod was exaggerated, so big that her face cracked into Ivy's chin. A little-girl giggle deflated some of the tension in the room as she wrinkled her little nose, then rubbed the bridge of it.

Jacob dared to look at Ivy. She was watching him. In that unguarded moment, there was wonder in her expression.

It kicked an extra beat into Jacob's heart. *What if they could?*

No. There were no what-ifs. He'd chosen his life and she'd chosen hers. He was still fueled by a need to serve others and she still lived in fear. Nothing could change that.

His time with Ivy had long passed, and she'd nailed the door shut by lying to him for nearly five years. Now they had to consider what was best for Wren, not for themselves.

"Bacon!" Wren's sudden shout made both of her parents jump. She wriggled in Ivy's arms, then looked over her shoulder at Jacob. "Jaycup has bacon. In the frijalator. Right?"

Ivy shot him an apologetic look. "She loves bacon."

"Like her—" *Like her daddy.* He cleared his throat to convince the hoarse emotion to tamp down. "Bacon in the refrigerator? Yes, I do. Want some?"

"Yes!" That shout was loud enough to set off a rock slide in the canyon.

This was the perfect excuse to walk away and focus on something else, to get his emotions in line. "Bacon it is." At least the kid knew what she wanted.

He turned toward the fridge.

On the counter, his phone buzzed.

Jacob reached for it instinctively. "Give me one second."

He glanced at the screen, and his jaw muscles tightened. It was Linc. Turn on TV. Breaking news. Second murder in SR. Law Office of Ivy Bridges.

"What's wrong?" Ivy stepped closer to Jacob but stopped short. She had no right to read his phone.

But the way his expression had shifted away from the wonder that had nearly derailed her heart as he interacted with Wren sent a shudder through her. In the time it took him to read that text, his eyebrows drew together and his attention completely left the room. Ivy's arms tightened around Wren as she turned to follow his gaze over her shoulder, half expecting to see the man with the US Marshal badge training a gun on her.

There was no one there.

Wren wriggled. "Too hard, Mama." She squirmed until Ivy set her down. Bounding into the living room, singing a song about butterflies and bullfrogs, she plopped her knees on the recliner and rocked the chair back and forth.

Jacob followed Wren, but he stopped at the end table and picked up the remote. He clicked on the TV, then stood with his arms crossed, watching the weather on the local television station.

Glancing at Wren to make sure she was occupied with the novelty of the rocking recliner, Ivy cautiously followed Jacob.

He didn't acknowledge her presence as he dropped the remote onto the chair. He just stared at the meteorologist, who was detailing a cold front and possible storms headed for the area that evening.

Surely the weather hadn't set off Jacob. She checked on Wren, who was still watching the outside world come to life, then inched closer to Jacob. Her elbow brushed his arm, but she didn't back off. "Did something happen?" Maybe it was about another case he was working and it had nothing to do with her.

Either way, it had to be something big to pull him away from Wren, given his initial reaction to meeting her.

He exhaled slowly and tilted his head toward hers, still watching the television that was mounted on the log wall above the stone fireplace. "There's been another murder."

Ivy stepped back at the low rumble of his words, and sat on the edge of the coffee table. Someone else was dead. Someone connected to her, or Jacob wouldn't be acting like this.

If it had made the regional news almost two hours away from Swift River, then it was big.

It was probably also something her daughter didn't need to see blaring on the television. "Wren." Ivy's voice cracked. She did her best to swallow with a dry mouth then tried again as her daughter turned and plopped her bottom on the chair. "Wren, go into the bedroom, find your backpack and change into your other clothes. Oh, and brush your teeth." Tooth-brushing alone should buy several minutes.

Wren screwed up her mouth like she was going to suggest an alternate idea, but then she slid to the edge of the chair and ran for the bedroom at full steam. She was going to be disappointed when she figured out there were no options for pants and shirts, only the single pair of emergency clothes left in her preschool backpack.

"Shut the door behind you," she called to the retreating figure. "We're guests in someone's house."

The door slammed in response.

Jacob and Ivy both jumped, and she looked up at him. "Who else is dead?" Did she really want to know? In all likelihood, more grief was about to break over her like a tidal wave.

"I don't know." He sat on the recliner, his knees touching hers as a commercial for a retirement community near Las Vegas blared over his shoulder. "Linc just told me to turn on the TV. But, Ivy?" He reached for her, hesitated, then took her hand in his. He stared down at their joined hands as his thumb brushed idly over hers.

Despite the situation, his touch sent tingles of remembrance up her arms and into her heart. He used to do that every time he held her hand, that absentminded touch that implied familiarity and belonging. In the space between them, a stillness hovered that the outside world couldn't touch. It was as if the universe drew down to the small space their hands occupied.

She was safe here. Safe with this man who had never truly vacated the home he'd occupied in her heart.

But their world was much bigger and much different than her heart wanted to believe.

Ivy withdrew her hands. Cold reality took the place of his warm touch. "Just tell me what's going on." She could take it.

Sitting back, Jacob rested his hands on his knees, digging his fingers into his legs as though he didn't trust himself not to reach for her again. "Someone was found dead in your office."

No. Ivy sagged. "You're sure?"

The television blared the intro theme for the morning news, a jarring soundtrack to the drama of her life.

Jacob stood and turned toward the screen. "I'm not sure of anything anymore."

She probably wasn't supposed to hear that.

Although she wanted to stand, too, she was certain her knees wouldn't let her. If there had been a murder in her office, then…

She swallowed a rising dread as the Swift River Savings and Loan building dominated the screen. The sandstone-and-brick building's image was nearly covered by a Breaking News banner.

Ivy gripped the arms of the chair. The windows for her office were on the second floor, right side. She pulled the remote from beneath her, where she'd sat on it earlier, and raised the volume as she glanced up the hall to make sure Wren wasn't finished dressing.

"…after the body was discovered. The Swift River Police Department has not released the victim's identity. They are searching for attorney Ivy Bridges, who has not been seen since yesterday afternoon and may have information pertinent to the case." The professional headshot from her website flashed on the screen. "Anyone with information on Ms. Bridges's whereabouts is asked to call the Swift River Police Department or the Dow County Sheriff's office."

"Mama! On TV!" Wren launched herself at Ivy, who barely caught her. When had she come back into the room? "That you!"

Ivy forced a smile, trying to reconcile the evil of this latest blow with the precious innocence of her daughter. "Yes, baby. Mama is on TV." She snuggled Wren close and stroked her hair, pouring out wordless prayers of protection for her daughter and her little-girl view of life. *Oh, God, please. Make this stop.*

"Bacon?" Wriggling free, Wren slid to the floor and made a run for the kitchen. "I get bacon."

Ivy rose to follow her daughter before she could drag the contents of Jacob's refrigerator onto the kitchen floor. Her hands shook. What did she do now?

Stepping in front of her, Jacob halted her progress. "Wren can't hurt anything in there. The only thing in the fridge is bacon and lunch meat." When she started to step around him, he moved with her. "We need to talk about what comes next. You have to contact the sheriff. Immediately."

"I know." She kept her eyes glued to the UNLV logo on his sweatshirt. Their college. Their time together. Once again, that twisting roller coaster of past and present threw off her equilibrium. Today's Jacob, a grown, battle-scarred stranger, tried to meld with past Jacob, the man who'd once promised her forever. That blend did not mix well with the threats to her life and now to her reputation. While the media hadn't labeled her a killer, there was no way anyone watching wouldn't automatically think it. "Am I a suspect?"

"No. But they need to know you're safe, and they have questions. You dropped your purse at the crime scene."

Her purse. It hadn't even crossed her mind again. "That makes me look guilty. I was there."

"It makes you look like a victim." When Ivy wavered, Jacob's hands found her elbows. "Linc will go with us. I'll call Angie to come to the cabin and stay with Wren. We can—"

"I'm not leaving Wren. Not even with your sister." A lightning bolt of panic ran from her head into her stomach. Separate from her daughter? Now? "I can't."

"You can't take Wren. It's too dangerous. I wouldn't

take you if I didn't have to. No one knows she's here. She's safe." His grip on her elbows tightened. "I will not let anything happen to—"

Ivy looked up in time to see the pain etched on his face. Jacob was Wren's father. Ivy was no longer the sole decision-maker in her daughter's life.

She couldn't even begin to process how that made her feel.

Something clattered to the floor in the kitchen. Jacob glanced in that direction, then turned his attention back to Ivy. "The ranch has security. If Angie needs them, they'll be here in an instant."

Another crash came from the kitchen. "Mama? I drop eggs."

Jacob winced. "I forgot about those."

Pulling from his grasp, Ivy turned to go help her daughter. She needed distance. Time to think. Things were moving too fast.

But Jacob laid a hand on her shoulder. "Ives, you really don't have a choice."

She stopped and turned her face toward the plank ceiling. He was right.

Maybe there wasn't a choice, but she could take control. Rather than knuckle under to fear and wait for those men to come at her again, she could take charge and see that they never hurt another person.

But taking charge meant taking actions that might appear foolish to the outside world. "I want my files on the Mendez case before I'm forced to turn them over. I need to know why someone's coming after me."

"They're not electronic?"

"I told you. Mr. Mendez had several old stock certificates and deeds that went back a few decades. I have hard copies. A couple of days ago, Clarissa brought a stack of paperwork to the house that I never got to look at. They're at my house in a safe under the bathroom sink in the upstairs hall."

His head jerked toward her. "The bathroom sink?"

"It's bolted through the floor joists. The original owners ran a pawn shop on Fifth Street. He wasn't taking any chances, I guess."

"Mama?" Wren's voice broke in from the kitchen. "I clean up."

Jacob's other eyebrow raised and his lips tipped slightly. "Mama will be there in a second." He sobered. "I don't know about you going back."

She wanted his help, not his authority. Needed him to back her up, not to call the shots. If she didn't regain some control soon, her emotions would fall to pieces, and her mind would fixate on who might be dead.

Either Marcie Burns, who cleaned the office two nights a week, or Kendra Thompkins, her admin assistant, had stepped into a situation Ivy should have warned them about. She should have called and let them know her life had been threatened. Instead, she'd fled, leaving them heedless of the danger around her.

And now, the blood of someone else she cared about was on her hands.

Backing away from Jacob, she headed for the kitchen. "We'll stop at my house on the way to see the sheriff. I want to end this."

She had to end this. Before anyone else was killed.

FOUR

If this had been a case he was working while on duty with the National Park Service, the actions he was taking would likely mean dismissal before they closed the file.

Jacob stepped aside on the dirt path that led away from a small park a couple of blocks from Ivy's house and held a branch aside so she could pass. She'd insisted they could get to her house without being seen if they used the small path through the narrow wooded area that passed behind her house.

As they walked slowly along a trail that could barely be called an animal path, he counted a long list of issues he'd call an agent on the carpet for if he was in charge, starting with allowing an endangered witness to call the shots.

So far, Linc hadn't said a word. He'd simply watched their backs as they'd rented a nondescript sedan and driven to Swift River. His friend was currently cruising by Ivy's house, looking for anything suspicious.

There was no telling what he was really thinking.

Stepping in Ivy's footsteps, Jacob said a quick prayer of thanks for Linc, first as a platoon sergeant overseas and now as a team leader. There were few other people in the world who would put up with what that man was putting up with today.

And Jacob was only putting up with this because it was Ivy. If he didn't do what it took to keep her safe, she would strike out on her own the minute his back was turned.

They wound along the path, away from the sounds of children at play. Through the trees to their left, an empty soccer field glistened in the March sunlight. To their right, barely visible through the new green leaves of spring, houses and privacy fences backed up to the small wooded area.

The warmth of the spring sun, the laughter of children and the neat avenue of homes painted a picture-perfect small-town slice of life.

But that slice was also home to two murderers. Jacob watched every shadow, certain that each held a threat.

"My place is about four houses away," Ivy said over her shoulder as she ducked beneath a limb. "Watch your head." She seemed to instinctively know every low-hanging bush and tripping vine. According to her, few knew the path existed. She and Wren walked it nearly every day, the little girl delighting in her "secret passage."

How he wished he could see that.

Actually, he wished he had time to process that he had a child, a gift he'd given up imagining he'd ever be blessed with. If he stopped to think, it was overwhelming. Knee-weakening.

Which was why he had to build a wall around his heart and keep walking. Because, right now, rather than adventuring with their daughter, Ivy was fighting for their lives.

In front of him, she soldiered on. He hoped she

couldn't see the sheer panic that was rising within him as a result of this whole escapade.

"Garcia, can you hear me?" Linc's voice came through his Bluetooth earbud. They'd activated a push-to-talk app on their phones in order to make communication easier.

Jacob pressed his screen. "Roger."

"I've cruised the block twice. Nobody seems to be watching the house. There's a vacant house for sale two doors down. I'm going to walk around it like I'm checking it out. Should be able to keep an eye out from there."

"Keep me posted."

Ivy stopped, and Jacob nearly ran into her. She pointed at a thin break in the trees and undergrowth, where an offshoot of the trail curved to the right. "That leads to my backyard."

Edging around her, Jacob took a knee, maintaining cover while surveilling her backyard. A play set rested near the neighbor's chain-link fence on one side. The wood-and-plastic swing set with a playhouse and a slide was ready for adventures.

Birds chirped in the distance, but not nearby. He and Ivy had disrupted the habitat. The sounds of children had dulled until only wisps of laughter drifted past.

Nearby, a car door slammed, probably Linc at the house down the street.

Ivy kneeled beside him, her shoulder brushing his. He'd tried all day to ignore how cute she looked trying to be incognito by wearing his Cardinals cap. So much of her personality remained like the woman he'd once loved, who geared up for softball games with her hair in a long braid.

Her dark hair was shorter now, but it still hung past her shoulders, swinging in a ponytail she'd pulled through the back of the cap. No matter how much he wanted to deny it, his heart still recognized her.

Yet he could never give her what she wanted. A solid family home, where the husband kept nine-to-five hours. Where the work didn't involve danger on a daily basis.

His love hadn't been enough to defeat her fear in the past. It wouldn't be enough now.

"It's still in one piece." Ivy's whisper broke through his thoughts, her voice so low he wasn't certain she meant for him to hear.

The magnitude of what she was going through pulled him out of his self-pity. This was more for Ivy than not knowing who lurked in the shadows or why they were hunting her. It was an attack on both aspects of her life, personal and professional. Even her own home wasn't safe.

She had to feel as adrift as he often felt, wondering where solid ground was in an ocean where his very identity as a soldier had been ripped away from him. Right now, Ivy didn't even have a change of clothes. Everything about her life was suspect and possibly dangerous.

He didn't know how to put his own storm-tossed emotions from the last couple of years into words, but he knew she had to be in pain, that her life had been threaded with an underlying anxiety that couldn't be caught by the tail and wrestled into submission.

He found her hand and squeezed. If only he could reassure her that he'd protect her and Wren from whatever fire-breathing dragons attacked. But he couldn't make that guarantee. The only thing he could offer was the silent promise that he'd stay beside her, that he'd sacrifice his own life to save theirs.

Right now, her years of silence didn't matter. Keeping her alive did.

"All clear." Linc's voice broke the moment. "I can't see inside, though. I'll keep up the charade and can be there quick if you need me."

"Going in." Jacob's heart pounded like it hadn't since his final patrol in Afghanistan. It was always an adrenaline rush going outside the wire, leaving safety to face potential combat. But this time?

He glanced at Ivy, who was watching him for the next move.

This time the personal stakes were so much higher.

He had to think like a soldier and a federal agent, not like a man who'd once loved a woman and who now had a child. He crept forward, motioning for Ivy to wait. "I'm going to clear the house. You should be safe here. Linc is within shouting distance. Run if you have to."

She wanted to argue. There was rebellion in the way she moved to stand and in the set of her jaw, but then she sank back on her heels. "Okay."

That was almost too easy, but he didn't have time to dwell on it.

Pulling his pistol from the holster at his hip, Jacob slipped across the yard, catching a glimpse of Linc, who was inspecting the chain-link fence at the other house.

Jacob climbed the deck steps. The back door was slightly ajar. "Door's open," he said, relaying the intel to Linc. "Keep an eye on Ivy." He hated to leave her behind, but bringing her into an unsecured house was more dangerous than having her hide on a trail that few knew existed.

The sunlit kitchen, bright with white cabinets and dark granite countertops, was a mess. The contents of every cabinet and drawer had been tossed onto the floor. Some-one had definitely been here searching.

He made his way around the corner, drawing on instinct and training. Listening, watching...

Silence. Nothing but oppressive, eerie silence.

The rest of the house had suffered the same fate as the kitchen. Clothes, pillows, books... Ivy's home had been reduced to debris scattered on the floor.

But the bathrooms were largely untouched. Jacob almost smiled as he holstered his pistol. Ivy was right. Nobody searched a bathroom for business files.

He waved her in and watched her run across the yard and up the steps. His heart ached for her and the destruction she was about to encounter. If only he could shield her.

Stopping inside the door, she took in the chaos. Her hand went to her mouth. Tears hung on her eyelashes.

Before Jacob could offer comfort, she breathed deeply and squared her shoulders. It was a move he'd seen often in the past, when she'd been a champion softball player. She'd shoved aside her feelings to focus on business. "I'll make this fast. Files, clothes, and out of here." She was gone before he could stop her.

She was right. This was a crime scene. He'd call the sheriff as soon as they were out, although her house was within the city limits and was officially under the police department's jurisdiction.

Jacob walked into the living room. Next to a cream-colored sofa, a matching chair lay on its side, colorful throw pillows spilling on the floor. A cheerfully painted wooden trunk overflowed with toddler toys.

Ivy thumped around upstairs. The house was bright

and cozy, every inch a reflection of her personality. It was the kind of home she'd always dreamed of.

A settled-down, never-have-to-leave-it home.

By the front door, a softball bat rested against the wall. He smiled. It was likely her main defense against possible intruders. Smart move. In Ivy's hands, a bat could do real damage.

Ivy had lived for softball season. For Christmas their junior year, Jacob had saved money to buy her a green DeMarini bat she'd been eyeing. The way she'd jumped up from her seat in front of the fireplace and thrown her arms around—

Wait.

Jacob shifted the bat, holding it so the barrel rested on his left palm and the grip rested on his right. DeMarini. Bright green. Pressing his lips together, he slid his right hand up the grip. Where the knob curved, there was a tiny scratched heart.

This was the bat he'd given her.

She'd kept it. Of all the bats she'd owned, this was the one that was handy to grab at a moment's notice.

Interesting. He wouldn't let his heart or his head read too deeply into that fact, though. Their time had passed. He'd caused her too much pain when he'd abandoned their future for the military. He'd never even called after he left, because he'd been certain that hearing her voice would wreck his resolve to do what he believed was right.

And now that she'd denied him the joy of his daughter's first four years of life, he wasn't certain he could ever trust her fully. That was a pain that had yet to be explored. He feared how it would cut when he let it sink in.

"I'm ready." Ivy's voice came from behind him.

Jacob turned. She stood at the foot of the stairs, holding a large backpack.

"You kept this?" *Seriously?* He hadn't intended to ask.

"I got rid of most of my bats, but I still play sometimes. This was the nicest one I owned." Wrapping her fingers around the barrel, she tugged it from his hands then propped it against the couch. "That's all."

Linc's voice hit Jacob's ear. "Police car. Get out. Now."

Grabbing Ivy's hand, Jacob tugged her to the back door, adrenaline surging in his veins. "Run. Don't look back."

As they burst out the back door, he tried to shield Ivy, tensed against a bullet.

She was fleeing her home. Her *refuge.*

Their feet pounded on the deck. *Oh, Lord, please don't let them hear us.* Ivy held tightly to the backpack slung across her shoulder. They crossed the yard faster than she'd run since sprints during practice in college, her knee shooting a flash of reminder that it had been surgically repaired once before because of activity like this. *Don't give out on me. Not now.*

They blasted into the woods. A tree branch whipped her arm with a burning lash.

Abruptly, Jacob stopped. His shoulders rose and fell with every deep breath. He did that slight head tilt that said Linc was talking in his earbud, then shook his head and pressed his phone screen. "No. Meet me at the place we designated."

Bouncing on her toes, Ivy watched over her shoulder. Shouldn't they be running? Surging panic urged her to shove Jacob out of the way and keep barreling up the path. She wasn't going to die behind her own house. She wasn't going to leave her daughter an orphan.

Wasn't going to leave Wren without telling her about her father.

She shifted the backpack higher on her shoulder, then shook her hands as though trying to fling the shudders that ran through her out the tips of her fingers.

Jacob's hands rested warm on her shoulders. "Ivy. It's okay. Linc said the guy is checking the house, not following us."

"Really?" Man, she hated the way her voice shook with the simple question.

No fear. That was how she had to get through this. *No fear. Be strong.* The greatest lesson her father had taught her. *Never let anyone know you're scared.*

That advice had led her to two division championships in college.

She breathed in twice… Three times. The faint scent of new leaves and something slightly minty that she'd come to recognize as either Jacob's shampoo or his soap sank into her lungs and brought calm.

He was here. He'd keep her safe. And she'd do her part to protect him as well.

"Linc was going to talk to him, but we can't risk connecting him to you or to me. We'll meet him at the strip mall by the highway as planned." Jacob started walking again. He reached back, holding his hand out behind him as though he wanted her to take it.

Ivy stared as she took several steps, then wrapped her fingers around his. It was the third time he'd offered his hand to her today.

And her fingers still fit perfectly in his. Somehow that both cut and comforted.

With a quick squeeze, he let go and pushed ahead through underbrush and branches, holding aside any that threatened to attack her as they passed. "He's circling the block and driving past the parking lot to make sure no one is hanging around."

Good. They weren't running blindly toward danger. Surely Linc would notice anything out of place.

Holding a branch, Jacob glanced back at Ivy then faced forward again. "I think we should hand the files off to Linc when we meet up with him."

Ivy gripped the strap of her backpack tighter. Was he kidding? They'd risked their lives for these files. She was planning to open them as soon as they were safely in the car. She wanted her life back. Wanted answers. Delay was out of the question.

"I can feel you stabbing me in the back with your eyes."

Of course he could. Even after all of their years apart, he knew her well enough to know she'd hate that idea. "After practically choking on my own stomach for the past ten minutes from the stress of breaking into my own house, I'd kind of like to keep them with me." *Her own house.* She'd never feel safe there again.

"I get that." He stopped a few feet from where the path opened up at the park and scanned the area, then turned. His eyes searched hers. "My biggest concern right now is getting you to the sheriff and then safely back home. My second biggest is getting those files to safety. I'd feel a whole lot better if my two biggest concerns weren't in the same vehicle." He glanced away, then pinned her gaze. "And frankly, I'd rather send the files with Linc than send you with Linc."

The breath caught in Ivy's throat. His words… His expression… His reluctance to let her go…

They all swept brushstrokes that painted one picture. He still cared.

Her heart urged her to lean into him. To seek the comfort and acceptance he had always offered, the dream he had once shared with her…at least until he'd chosen a different dream. One that involved danger and death at every turn.

The same dream that had killed her father. And his new career path was no better. He still faced the same sorts of criminals who'd gunned down her father on that joint-task-force mission.

It was the one way of life she openly feared. He'd chosen it. She couldn't follow.

End of story.

She looked away, over his shoulder at the light at the end of the path.

The laughter of a group of little girls who sat in the dirt beneath the swings drifted into their hiding place. Had it only been a couple of days ago when she'd watched Wren play on those very swings? It had all been so mundane. So normal. She'd never expected her routine to change.

Now, her life had been ripped off the axis It might never be put back together again.

"You ready? It's clear." Jacob reached back and grabbed her wrist, pulling her forward.

Ivy nodded and fell into step behind him. This was her life now. Running. Hiding. Trying not to faint in panic.

As they neared the small parking lot, one of the mothers at a nearby picnic table laughed.

The sound pinged Ivy's recognition. Joely Davidson, the wife of Swift River Police Chief Cade Davidson. She sat with her back to Ivy, watching her young granddaughter sweep down the slide.

Ivy ducked her head and pulled her ball cap lower. If Chief Davidson's officers were involved in Clarissa's death, Ivy didn't need Joely to see her skulking around the park. The officers would know she'd been to her house and had the files. Anyone searching for her would double-down on their efforts.

She dared to glance toward the ladies again. April Cassidy was watching Ivy and Jacob with a furrowed brow.

If Ivy had been sitting in her spot, she'd have been suspicious, too. Two adults sneaking out of the woods carrying a backpack?

This did not look good.

April leaned across the table and motioned for her companions to move closer.

"Jacob," Ivy said through gritted teeth as she stepped beside him and linked her arm with his, resting her head on his shoulder. "We have to get out of here. Fast."

His pace picked up, no questions asked. Only trust.

"Not too fast." She gripped his arm tighter. "We have an audience. Put your arm around me. Do something to make us look less like criminals and more like we're out for a sweet little stroll."

His arm slid around her waist as though they walked like this every day.

They had. Once.

Ivy tucked into his side and kept her face away from the women, grateful for Jacob's baseball cap. They ambled across the grassy area between the woods and the parking lot.

Joely wouldn't hesitate to call her husband and report

suspicious goings-on at the playground. She'd called him on casual hunches before. This had better look convincing.

It sure *felt* convincing. In the same way her fingers had twined with his as though the years hadn't passed, this position, with his arm around her protectively and her head on his shoulder, was achingly familiar and... devastatingly right.

At the edge of the parking lot, Jacob's grip on her waist tightened. His entire body tensed. "I need you to do exactly what I tell you."

Every muscle in Ivy's body froze. She stumbled on the asphalt. "What?"

He laughed, the sound too fake and too loud, and helped her right herself, then wrapped both arms around her and pulled her to his chest, standing between her and their rental car about twenty feet away. Leaning closer, he laid his cheek against hers.

What was he doing? Her heart pounded. Whether it was fear or something else, she couldn't tell. Her mind was too busy trying to fit his words and his actions together. They didn't mesh.

His lips brushed her ear. "I think someone is in the car."

Ivy dug her teeth into her lower lip to keep from whimpering in fear or screaming in frustration. None of this was easy. Why couldn't she just go to the police like a normal person?

Because someone dressed as a police officer and driving a police cruiser had tried to kill her.

Her breath shook. "Okay."

With a smile so fake everyone for fifty miles had to realize it, Jacob pressed a kiss to her forehead and directed her toward the paved walkway that circled the park, away from the playground and the parking lot. He was quiet, likely working through their situation in his head.

His silence and their slow place were maddening. For all she knew, a sniper had them in his sights.

All she wanted to do was run. Her entire being ached to race up the once-safe little dirt path to her house. Surely, if she buried her head beneath her pillows, she'd wake up and discover this was a horrific nightmare.

"Here's what we'll do." When Jacob spoke, his voice was low, although no one was near. "I saw someone move in the back, like they were shifting position. Hopefully they don't realize I saw. That stand of trees to the left opens up onto a neighborhood street, correct?"

"Meadow Street."

Jacob repeated the words, then listened to his earbud. "We're going to walk through those trees and meet Linc on the other side. You're going with him and I'm going to double back to the car. If we have one of our bad guys where we want him, then I—"

"Jacob, no." She wasn't an expert in criminal law, but she could see where he was headed. While he had no actual jurisdiction over her case or in Swift River, he could argue it was a citizen's arrest if he managed to take their possible assailant into custody.

He could also get killed.

"Yes." Her urged her to walk faster. "If I can end this right now, I will."

Through the trees, Linc's truck turned the corner off Mesa and cruised up Meadow.

Ivy dug in her heels, literally and metaphorically. "Let Linc help you. I'll lay on the floorboards of his truck out of sight while—"

"Whoever's in the car could have an accomplice. You

and Linc are getting out of range, and I'm going after this guy."

"Jacob—" Her voice was desperate, but she didn't care. He couldn't do this.

He stopped and turned her to face him, pinning her with a look that said he wouldn't let her argue any longer. "You'll stay in range of comms. Linc will know if I need help." The commanding expression softened, and his voice dropped low, and took on a pleading tone. "Please. So I know you're safe. Think about Wren."

She wanted to argue, to protect him, but he was right. Her daughter—their daughter—needed to come first.

No matter the cost.

"Run straight to Linc's truck. No looking back. I'll see you as soon as we have this guy in custody and the sheriff takes him." His eyes scanned hers, then he dipped his head and brushed a kiss against her lips.

He pulled away and turned her toward Linc's truck before jogging off.

Back into danger.

FIVE

As soon as he heard the truck accelerate away from the curb, Jacob took his first full breath in nearly two minutes. Ivy was relatively safe, and he could focus on handling whoever was lying in wait in the back seat of their rental car. The closer he walked to the vehicle, the hotter his anger flared. How dare someone come after Ivy this way? How dare they threaten her, terrify her…?

Try to kill her.

Ivy and he may have a lot to sort out in their personal lives, but she was still one of the most incredible people he'd ever been blessed to know, the one woman he had never truly been able to let go of. She did not deserve this.

She deserved the life she'd built for Wren, the one with the colorful throw pillows and the backyard swing set and the enchanted path to the park.

The life he'd once wanted, too.

His pace increased. This ended now.

When he'd seen that shadow shift and the top of a head appear briefly in the back seat behind the driver's side, he'd nearly grabbed Ivy on instinct and run back the way they'd come.

He clenched and unclenched his fists, working hard

not to reach for his concealed Glock too soon. It would be nice if he didn't need it at all. If he could just surprise the person in the car enough to shock them into surrender.

There was no way it would be that easy.

Likely, he was headed into a full-on war.

His adversary had better cover by virtue of being inside the vehicle. With no other cars in the lot and few trees on this side of the park, Jacob had no cover close enough to protect himself.

He slowed his approach, watching the vehicle.

At the playground, the small group of women and children that Ivy had called attention to earlier had packed their things and were walking across the soccer field. They were on the far side of the park, past where Ivy and Jacob had come out of the trees. Another small wooded area on the far side of the soccer field was thin enough to reveal houses on the other side.

Good. They were headed home. Jacob didn't have to worry about catching a child in any potential cross fire.

Lord, please don't let there be any cross fire.

From this angle, the midday sunlight reflected off the car's back window, partially obstructing his view. Jacob's heart pounded. His mind spun through tactical advantages and disadvantages.

There were no advantages. Nothing but a wide-open parking lot and empty space between him and a potential killer.

A killer who was probably getting antsy if he'd seen them coming earlier. It had been several minutes since Jacob redirected Ivy. Whoever was in the vehicle had to be wondering where they were and what was taking them so long.

As he approached, Jacob scanned the ground under

the car. No one had rolled beneath the sedan. There were no bushes or trees that could offer concealment within fifty feet of the vehicle. There was no way someone could catch him by surprise from outside that car.

His concern lay inside.

When he was ten feet from the vehicle, Jacob walked even slower, allowing his footfalls to roll silently on the asphalt. He glanced around the neighborhood streets and the park. No one was visible.

It was just him and the end of Ivy's nightmare.

Raising his weapon, he stopped about six feet from the vehicle. "Federal agent!" The sound of his voice rang off the trees and houses. "Show me your hands!"

Silence. Even the birds stopped singing, as though startled by his command.

Nothing moved in or around the vehicle.

Easing closer, he stepped so that the rear passenger side pillar behind the back window was between him and any potential shot from inside the vehicle. It was scant cover, but it was all he had. If nothing else, it would make the intruder's shot angle too awkward for deadly accuracy. "Show me your hands!"

Still nothing.

Working hard not to hold his breath, he inched toward the vehicle, muscles tight against a possible assault. When he was as close as he dared, he pulled the door open quickly and aimed at the back seat.

No one was there.

The front seat was empty as well, though the driver's side back door hung slightly open, evidence that someone had recently evacuated the vehicle. Likely, they realized Jacob had spotted them.

Holstering his weapon, Jacob scanned the park. The

guy had to be moving fast, because Jacob had only been distracted by getting Ivy to safety for a minute, maybe two.

The bushes, the playground and the nearby picnic pavilion all seemed to be empty. He walked toward the play area, watching the tree line.

A figure dressed in jeans, a baseball cap and a dark shirt stood at the head of the small trail, watching Jacob. When he realized he'd been spotted, he turned and fled, disappearing deeper into the cluster of trees.

Jacob ran, every thud of his feet on the ground jarring his insides and reminding him of his past injuries, of his failures that day.

He couldn't fail this time.

Jacob burst into the trees. The branches and undergrowth he'd so carefully held aside for Ivy slapped him in the face and tripped him at his ankles. He stumbled over a root and narrowly avoided ripping out his eye on a rogue branch.

He couldn't see the figure except in brief snatches between limbs, but Jacob was gaining as the man crashed through the woods.

And then there was silence.

They weren't quite to Ivy's house. Where had he…?

A tree branch caught Jacob in the chest, knocking the air from his lungs. He stumbled backward and fell on the path, his hip taking the brunt of the impact as he landed hard on a tree root, shooting white-hot pain through his entire body.

Training and muscle memory had his pistol up and aimed toward his attacker before he'd even run through all of his options.

But the dark figure was gone, crashing away through

the underbrush toward Ivy's. By the time Jacob scrambled to his feet, two car doors slammed and tires squealed as a vehicle rushed out of the neighborhood.

Through the trees, Jacob could see the flash of the car as it passed the house he was behind.

It was a Swift River PD cruiser, the blue-and-black emblem on the Dodge Charger a blur as the vehicle streaked up the street.

Sinking against a tree, Jacob holstered his pistol. He leaned forward and braced his hands on his knees, fighting to catch the breath that had been forced from his chest. When his lungs felt like they were at capacity again, he straightened and rubbed his hand across the ache in his ribs, turning from side to side until he was relatively certain nothing was broken. That was going to hurt worse tomorrow, along with his hip.

What hurt more was the fact that he'd lost their chance at taking custody of a suspect. At putting an end to the terror being constantly hurled in Ivy's direction.

Not only had he failed, but he'd also been spotted. The killer had seen his face, had even managed to draw Linc out of hiding when he'd shown himself to pick up Ivy.

This was a huge failure.

The day was half over. They hadn't accomplished their singular mission of getting Ivy safely to the sheriff's office, and it seemed things were moving more quickly toward disaster.

Jacob started walking back toward the parking lot, working hard not to favor his hip. No matter what happened next, they were going straight to the sheriff, who'd likely have some choice words for Jacob after this fiasco. What he really wanted to do was have Linc floor that truck and get Ivy out of Swift River as fast as the engine on that huge pickup of his would let him.

But that would likely get Ivy into deeper trouble with law enforcement, and the last thing he needed was for someone to decide she was a suspect in hiding. If a warrant was issued, he'd have no say in what happened to her, no say in how to protect her.

Their only choice was to walk straight into the fire. To go to the sheriff, even though Ivy's assailants knew she was in town.

And with the danger escalating, there really was no good way to shield Ivy from a killer intent on striking.

Ivy swiped her slick palms against the legs of her blue jeans and pulled her collar away from her throat. The white walls and dark carpet in the hallway at the Dow County Sheriff's office seemed to stretch longer and longer, as though she'd been stepped through the fictional Looking Glass with Alice. If her quaking knees didn't drop her before they reached the sheriff's door, she'd be shocked.

And grateful.

Walking down the hall with Jacob felt like whiplash. Less than an hour earlier, she'd left him behind so he could run toward danger. Time had slowed to a crawl in the few minutes it had taken him to reestablish contact with Linc.

The man had escaped, but when they picked up Jacob safely at the corner of Pierce and Sunset, that hadn't mattered. Ivy had wanted to jump from the truck while it was still rolling and throw herself into his arms. She hadn't realized the desire had been beneath the surface since the first moment she looked him in the eye the night before.

Instead, she'd remained in the truck and planted her hands beneath her thighs, shoving that urge into the deepest parts of her heart. He didn't need to know how much those few minutes had terrified her.

He also didn't need to know much she was starting to remember their past dreams of a home and a future together.

With a long look that seemed to read Ivy's thoughts, Linc had taken the files and walked back to their rental car. He'd exchange the vehicle for another and would meet them at the ranch.

Jacob had been grim as he watched Linc walk away with Ivy's backpack slung across his shoulder. The situation was growing more desperate by the moment. How was this her life?

As much as she wanted to hide under her bed, Ivy had bitten down on fear and made a call to the sheriff to let him know they were coming. She'd ridden silently to the office, an imposing structure on the outskirts of the county seat in Landow, about twenty miles from Swift River. The newer brick building held offices, a training center and the county detention center.

Ivy prayed no one inside wanted her dead.

They followed the woman who had introduced herself as Deputy Davis while Ivy tried to keep from dropping to the floor like overboiled spaghetti noodles. There were very few deputies in the hallway or in the rooms lining it, but Ivy tried to take in every one of their faces, their postures. While the uniformed man who had fired at her had been driving a Swift River Police Department cruiser and had been wearing a PD uniform, she couldn't stop herself from searching for a foe among the friendly.

"See anything?" Jacob leaned close over her shoulder, his breath warm against her ear.

That was an entirely different reason for her heart to jump into overdrive. His presence was much too real. Much too protective. Much too comforting.

The longer he walked toward danger with her, the more her feelings amped to levels she thought she'd squelched years ago. Levels she certainly didn't need to feel for him.

"Ivy?" He laid his hand on her shoulder. "Did you recognize anyone?"

"No."

They stopped in front of a door that bore a plaque etched with the name Sheriff Brandt Stanton. Deputy Davis knocked twice, then shoved open the door and ushered Ivy and Jacob inside.

The click of the door closing nearly broke Ivy. She'd never been claustrophobic, but the walls closed in and the air in the room fled. A thin sheen of sweat coated her skin. She was inexplicably hot and cold at the same time. And her body simply forgot how to breathe with rhythm.

Ivy forced herself to look around the office, tried to take in her surroundings instead of drowning in her rising panic. The room was plain, painted the same color as the hall. Several plaques hung on the wall beside an aerial map of the county. A coffee maker sat on a file cabinet beside a bookcase behind the desk. Two chairs with burgundy cushions sat in front of it. The office had no personality, nothing to indicate the sheriff lived a life outside of his job.

It made sense. The less outsiders knew about his personal life, the better. Even she had no photos of Wren in her office or on social media. The world was a scary place.

She should know.

The sheriff stood and extended his hand, first to Ivy, then to Jacob. "Sheriff Brandt Stanton." He tipped his chin toward the chairs. "Have a seat."

She'd seen him around the courthouse a few times but had never interacted with him. Though he was in his sixties, he looked younger. His dark hair held little salt. Fit and tall, he coached rec ball on the weekends at a local church. While Ivy hadn't grown up in Swift River, she'd heard tales of the basketball team's epic state-championship run when he was in high school. He was friendly and helpful, but his demeanor also commanded respect.

When they were seated, he eyed Ivy as though he was trying to gauge her trustworthiness. "I appreciate you coming in person, Ms. Bridges. A lot of serious things are happening in your life right now, including the accusations you've made against law enforcement."

Ivy clenched her back teeth, fear scattering at the skepticism in the sheriff's voice. She counted to ten, praying silently that God would help her not to speak with the ire that rose at the hint she might not be fully truthful.

To his credit, Jacob said nothing, though his hands tensed on his knees. He wouldn't step over her or cut in unless she asked.

This was her wheelhouse, and she appreciated him letting her take the lead instead of assuming she was too weak to handle it.

"Sheriff Stanton." Ivy slid to the edge of the chair, lasering her gaze onto the older man's. "As I told you on the phone, I was attacked at Clarissa Mendez's home moments after I found…" Her anger slipped and fell away. Clarissa was dead. And someone in her office was dead and she still didn't know who.

Grief rose unexpectedly, choking her. Holding up a hand, she wrestled herself into composure. If she was going to help find the killer who was threatening her and her daughter, she had to appear calm and rational. The last thing she needed was to be dismissed as an *emotional woman*.

She took a deep breath and started again. "A man wearing a deputy marshal badge threatened me at the Mendez home. He physically assaulted me." She pulled her shirt collar away from her neck, revealing the bruises she'd spent long moments studying in the mirror this morning.

Bruises that could have squeezed the life from her body if she hadn't been able to fight back.

"Yes, I left the scene of a murder, but there were extenuating circumstances and there is no law against it. Before I could call nine-one-one, I was pulled over by a man in a Swift River police vehicle. A man in uniform who opened fire on my vehicle with a firearm that was not standard issue for one of their officers." She'd managed to deliver her speech with a steady voice, but only by the grace of God. "The bullets are still in the liftgate of my SUV."

Sheriff Stanton sat back and crossed his arms over his chest. The chair creaked. He shifted his gaze to Jacob. "We'll need that vehicle, though given the circumstances, it will only lead us to the shooter. At this point, I'm not sure any evidence in it will help in court." Sitting forward, he grabbed a tablet and swiped the screen to unlock it, then passed it to Ivy. "I had one of our admins obtain photos of the male members of the Swift River PD. Do you think you could recognize the man who shot at you? Start there, and then we'll get your official statement and get you somewhere safe."

So he believed her, despite his earlier comment about her accusations against law enforcement. Or at least he was pretending to. If those men were truly lawmen and the sheriff believed them over her, this could all be a ruse to take her into custody...or worse.

She'd run with what she had. "I'm not sure." She scrolled through the photos, but none of them sent a shiver down her spine. "Outside of a few of the officers I've seen incidentally around town or in the courthouse, these men aren't familiar. He was average height. Messy brown hair. Sunglasses. But honestly, I was more focused on the gun." A typical reaction, but it was a mistake she knew better than to make.

"That's how you knew it wasn't a department-issued weapon. Good job. It helps a bit." The sheriff took the tablet and set it aside on his desk. "Given there's possible police involvement, state investigators will be called in. I've been in contact with federal law enforcement as well and will send them your statement." He ran his hand down his cheek and crossed his arms again, staring at something on the wall behind Ivy. "Never imagined we'd encounter something like this in Dow County. Two murders in twelve hours? Hasn't happened in all of my years here."

For the first time, the magnitude of the situation hit Ivy. The danger had been so immediate, so personal, that she hadn't thought outside of herself, Clarissa and Wren. If either of those men was truly who they'd pretended to be, then their treachery could create ripples that started in Swift River and grew into tidal waves across the country.

Having a freak-out meltdown in the middle of the sheriff's office was not going to help anything. She drew her thinking back into this room and this moment. Back to her own questions, the ones that tore at her heart. "Sheriff, who was found in my office this morning?"

His expression softened. "I understand your concern, but I can't release that information yet. Swift River PD is in charge of that investigation and it's ongoing."

"I just want to know that Kendra Thompkins and Marcie Burns are safe."

Tapping his index finger on his chest, Sheriff Stanton nodded thoughtfully. "The initial nine-one-one call was made by a Marcie Burns late last night."

Ivy exhaled through pursed lips and let her eyes slip shut, but relief was not yet complete. She wanted to jump across the desk and shake the sheriff until he told her Marcie was safe, but he didn't seem like the type of man to be bullied. He wasn't torturing her with his silence. He was likely considering what he could safely say.

Finally, he spoke. "Mrs. Thompkins has called here twice this morning in reference to the Clarissa Mendez case, wanting to know if we've located you."

Ivy's muscles sagged until she practically melted into the chair. Those closest to her, the ones she'd inadvertently drawn into the line of fire, were safe. "Please let her know I'm fine."

The sheriff nodded. "We retrieved your purse from the Mendez home if you'd like to take it with you. You'll have to let us know if anything is missing."

Her purse. She'd nearly forgotten it even existed. Again. "Thank you."

The sheriff turned his attention to Jacob. "Special Agent Garcia, I don't have all of the facts yet, but we're assuming the Mendez murder and the death at Ms. Bridges's office are connected. We're working with the SRPD." His expression darkened. He flicked a glance at Ivy that blew away her relief like a summer rainstorm. "I'm hearing rumblings I don't like out of them, but all I can say right now is this—get Ms. Bridges to safety. This may be worse than any of us imagined."

SIX

"Mama!"

As soon as Ivy walked through the door of Jacob's cabin, Wren bounced up from a giant pile of pillows that dominated the floor in front of the fireplace. Clearly, she'd been watching TV.

Wren was in Ivy's arms almost before she could brace herself. "Mama! Watch *Bross* with Annie!" Her daughter bounced up and down, wriggling until Ivy settled her on her feet again. She bounded back to her pillows and plopped herself onto the cushions, where her new friend, Jacob's sister, was just now standing up. "Pway, pwease!"

Ivy's arms felt empty. For two hours, she'd leaned forward in the seat of the pickup truck, straining to get back to Wren. She'd wanted to hold on to her precious baby girl until time stopped and the memories of the day faded. To let Wren's warmth and enthusiasm recharge her heart after a day filled with near misses and reawakening feelings. To know they were both safe, if only for a few minutes before the next curveball arrived.

But, as usual, Wren had her own schedule to keep, and sitting still with her mama wasn't on the agenda.

She tugged on Angie's pants leg and pointed at the TV. "*Bross*. Pwease."

Angie glanced at Ivy with a sheepish grin, then held up the remote in silent question.

On the television, Bob Ross, the soft-voiced painter, was frozen in place with his brush on a fluffy cloud, waiting for his pause to end.

"Play on." With a nod of assent, Ivy walked the rest of the way into the living room and dropped onto the couch. Honestly, her bones were just too tired to hold her up any longer. "Thanks for watching her on short notice. Jacob told me you took some time off from work."

"I needed the break." Angie waved a dismissive hand. "Doing my day job is a lot. I'm working on a team that's studying climate change and trying to determine how multimodel ensembles should be designed to help make future projections."

"I understood none of that."

"Half the time, I wonder if I do." Chuckling, Angie restarted Wren's television show. "And these days, trying to do that job while converting the ranch to a research-and-retreat center is worse."

"How's that going?" It was nice to talk about something normal.

"Pretty good. We're modeling after the North Rim Ranches, which are working to restore land near here that was overgrazed. We're allowing guests to come in if they're artists or scientists, so it's a unique situation. Trying as we get started, but fun." Angie put the remote on the mantel beneath the TV, then stepped gingerly over the pillows and a happily engrossed Wren and sat down on the opposite end of the couch from Ivy. "Where's Jacob?

When he called earlier, he said you were going to come up to the main house to stay with me."

"Thanks for that. He feels like it's less of a mess up there since he's doing reno here." That and it would put some distance between them.

Kind of like the distance Angie had put between them when she sat. It was a far cry from their college days at UNLV. Back then, they'd been close friends, slipping into the role of sisters-in-law that they were certain would come in their near future. After Jacob and Ivy parted, things had been awkward between the women, and they'd gradually drifted apart. They'd shared a brief hug this morning when Angie arrived to spend the day with a still sleepy-eyed Wren, but there hadn't been time for big reunions.

Now, they were face-to-face for the first time in five years. It was a strange, out-of-step feeling, looking at someone who used to know her so well, but who was now a stranger. Their lives no longer followed the same path, and they certainly hadn't followed the dreams Ivy and Jacob had shared.

Ivy jerked her head to the side in an attempt to reset her rogue thoughts. "Jacob is outside. He's on the phone with Linc making sure he's safely headed this way. He took a more circuitous route back." Unsure of how much Angie knew about the situation, Ivy chose her words carefully.

"Linc's coming here?" Angie tugged her auburn hair into a ponytail and dropped it again, then pulled the curtain back to glance out the window.

"Eventually."

"Hmm." Letting the curtain fall back into place, Angie

angled on the couch to watch Wren. "He never comes out to the ranch anymore."

Clearly, Angie knew Linc fairly well. Something in the tone of her voice said his absence bothered her.

Interesting.

Tugging at the hem of her shirt, Ivy glanced at the door, where the hum of Jacob's voice filtered through, though it was impossible to make out any actual words.

Linc needed to hurry. She wanted to get her hands on those files, to see what was there that could possibly be worth killing for, worth threatening an innocent four-year-old child for. They had expected Linc to be about an hour behind them, but Jacob was in full investigator mode and wanted to be sure Linc was on schedule.

And when Jacob finished his phone call and walked through that door...

Ivy watched Wren stare contentedly up at the calm-inducing painter on the television screen, as he swirled pink clouds into a blue sunset sky.

As though she could feel her mother watching, Wren looked over her shoulder and scrunched her face in her closest imitation of a wink, then returned to her happy viewing. Those eyes were so much like Jacob's. And unlike when they'd briefly come face-to-face this morning, Wren was fully awake and alert now.

How would this meeting go, when they had time to spend more than thirty seconds concentrated on one another?

And when should Ivy tell Wren who Jacob really was to her? She was barely four, but she was old enough to understand what a daddy was. She'd asked more than once why there wasn't a daddy living with them.

Ivy probably ought to be ashamed at how many times

she'd deflected that question with an offer of cookies or ice cream.

Now? The truth needed to be brought into the open.

Ivy's heart threatened to beat right out of her chest. *God, please help me with this. And help Jacob and me to know the right time to tell Wren the truth. Help Wren be ready to hear it.*

She cleared her throat, grasping for something to say to Angie, a *present* conversation to take her mind off a *future* conversation she'd never allowed herself to truly consider or plan for. "How did Wren do today?"

"She was great. We had breakfast, then had a tea party." Angie reached across the middle couch cushion and laid her hand on Ivy's wrist, grinning. "She was amazed by Jacob's tea stash."

"I'll bet." Wren loved a good tea party, and she'd seen the inside of Jacob's cabinet last night. The man was a connoisseur.

"She's a smart kid. We wandered around the yard for a while, then ate lunch. It took me a few minutes to figure out what she meant when she started pointing at the TV and asking for *'Bross,'* but we worked it out. She started an episode where he was painting a cabin in the mountains and fell asleep before he'd introduced his first 'happy little tree.' She only woke up about thirty minutes ago."

Ivy's smile was finally genuine. At four years old, her daughter was a diehard fan of the painter's soothing voice. She generally chose a streamed episode of *Bross* over every other form of entertainment. It was a nightly ritual for the two of them to snuggle on the couch and watch him paint an iconic nature scene before bedtime. More than once, Ivy had oohed and aahed over finger-

painted creations meant to mimic the soft-spoken painter's works or watched Wren draw at her whiteboard easel,
rhapsodizing about *twees* and *cwouds*. "I should have
thought to tell you that. *Bross* entertains her when nothing else will. Good job deciphering that."

"I've spent lots of time in the church nursery." Angie
withdrew her hand and sat back against her corner of
the couch, watching Wren. "Can I ask you a question
about her?"

Something in Angie's tone tweaked Ivy's anxiety. Her
mouth went dry. They hadn't told Angie about Wren's
relation to Jacob this morning. Ivy had been so focused
on Jacob meeting Wren and then on the horrible news
out of Swift River that she hadn't considered how Angie
was Wren's aunt. That she might see the resemblance.
That she, too, might resent Ivy for—

"Linc is good." The door slammed behind Jacob and
suddenly he was in the room.

Ivy jumped, and both women turned to look at him.

"He should be here sometime after sundown."

He pocketed his phone as he strode toward the kitchen,
not looking in their direction. "He thought he might have
picked up a tail about an hour outside Swift River, so he
wandered a bit more than he'd planned." He disappeared
around the corner and she could no longer see him.

Ivy whipped her gaze back to her daughter, who had
abandoned her *Bross* and was looking in Jacob's direction with narrowed eyes. Outside of one of her preschool
teachers and the occasional father in the church nursery,
Wren really hadn't been around a lot of men. Ivy hadn't
dated since her daughter was born. It hadn't seemed fair
to bring another man into Jacob's daughter's life.

Her insides churned. She scrubbed her hands along

the thighs of her borrowed jeans, trying to ground herself in something other than her wildly spinning emotions. A vise around her chest constricted her breathing to short gasps.

She couldn't do this. This was even harder than introducing them this morning. That had been a necessity. This was different somehow. Heavier. More emotional for all of them.

The way the pressure was building inside of her, she might explode before Jacob ever came out of the kitchen.

Why was he hiding in the kitchen?

"Ivy?" Angie's whisper came from far away.

At the weight of Angie's warm hand on her shoulder, Ivy jolted. She still couldn't catch her breath. Spots danced before her eyes.

"Take a deep breath. Whatever's going on, I'm praying for you." Angie's gentle voice cut through the roar in her ears. She ran her hand up and down Ivy's spine, pulling her out of the screaming voices in her head. "You're safe right now. No one is going to hurt you."

Ivy nodded, but she couldn't squelch the feeling that she needed to grab Wren and run out the front door, fast and far, to find the balance in their lives again and to keep from causing Jacob more pain.

Pain. That's why he was hiding.

Her panic ebbed as quickly as it had rushed in. This was not about her. This was about Jacob. About the daughter he was just now getting to know. She couldn't begin to imagine what he was feeling.

Sitting straighter, Ivy stood, then reached down and squeezed Angie's hand. She had to go to him, had to tell him it would all be okay. That Wren would love him. That he belonged in her life.

Because she couldn't hurt him any longer. Couldn't bear to think of his stomach in knots and his heart in tatters.

She had to release part of her daughter to Jacob, even if it complicated everything.

What was he thinking? Jacob braced his hands against the granite on either side of the kitchen sink and stared out the window into the trees that surrounded the cabin. On the other side of those trees, a deep ravine dropped off and led straight to the canyon not too far away.

His stomach felt as though he'd plummeted over the edge into free fall.

He was a grown man, and he was terrified of a four-year-old little girl.

His four-year-old little girl.

But really, was it fear of her? Or fear of what might happen when she got to know him? What if she was afraid of him? Didn't bond with him? Outright rejected him?

The fir trees that separated the private areas of the ranch from the public areas that the conservation team was developing swayed a wild dance, driven by the dark clouds that were beginning to peek over the horizon. While the previous day had featured driving rain, the line of storm clouds headed their way looked like they might pack more of a punch.

Angie had warned him that morning. This much rain suddenly on dry land could lead to flash flooding and rock slides.

But even his sister couldn't predict or explain the storm that had blown him off course just now, away from the living room, where his daughter was waiting, and into the kitchen, where he'd turned into a quaking mess.

What if he couldn't bond with Wren? Or he didn't know how to be a father?

He'd thought the hard part was over. He'd seen Wren this morning. Had rested a hand on her back and felt that heart-tugging, sleepy-little-kid warmth under his palm. She hadn't run away screaming.

But that was just the beginning, and things had moved so quickly in the aftermath. There had been no time to process what he felt. He'd had to shelve this brand-new fatherhood into a separate compartment while he worked through the day to protect Ivy and to search for answers.

But now? For the first time since he'd laid eyes on his little girl, he was standing still. There was no more running from the tidal wave of emotions. It had washed over him and threatened to slam him onto the beach. Too much...too fast.

From the living room, the quiet voice of Bob Ross and his there-are-no-mistakes philosophy of life drifted in.

Really, Bob? Because I've made some whopper mistakes. Big ones.

In grief over the loss of his father, he'd made the choice to turn his back on his college education and join the army. To not enter as an officer but as an enlisted infantryman. And he'd volunteered to bring up the rear on a patrol, leaving him as the lone survivor of his squad.

The choice to leave Ivy behind.

He dropped his chin to his chest. A red pottery bowl in the sink held the melted remains of chocolate ice cream and two spoons.

Angie had shared ice cream with his daughter.

His daughter.

How is this possible, God? The most heartrending thing the docs had said to him after a million tests at Brooke Army Medical Center was that he'd sustained internal injuries severe enough to prevent him from having children. He'd prepared himself for that future. It was one of the reasons he'd never reached out to Ivy again after he returned to Arizona. She needed a husband with a stable, safe job, and she wanted a family.

She'd started their family without him. Was he thrilled or angry?

Or awed? Only a few feet away, a little girl sat in front of the television watching Bob Ross paint a landscape, the same way he had as a kid. A little girl who carried his DNA when he'd never imagined he'd know such a gift.

Gripping the counter until his fingers pulsed with pain, he tensed until every muscle ached. How was he supposed to feel? There wasn't a battle plan for this, no guidance for a soldier who'd walked away from one future, had another blown to pieces and who had started working on Plan C. There was no chain of command to give him orders, to tell him how to approach a daughter to whom he was a stranger.

And there were no rules of engagement for her mother, who, he was beginning to realize, was still lodged in the secret rooms of his heart.

It was enough to make him want to saddle his horse, Shiloh, and ride until both of them dropped. He couldn't grasp one change before another blew by.

"Jacob." Ivy's low voice brushed his ears at the same time her warm hand rested between his shoulder blades.

She'd followed him, just like she had the night before.

She stood beside him and rested her forehead against his shoulder. Her hand remained on his back while her free hand slid down his arm until she found his fingers and held on tight.

Jacob drew his lips between his teeth and clamped down hard as the memories washed over him like the rain that would come with that storm on the horizon. The night the call came that his father had died, he'd fled his dorm room and headed for the football field, lost and angry. She'd found him by the bleachers and offered her silent support in this exact same way. One hand on his back to hold him up, the other wrapped around his, offering comfort. No words, just unwavering, unconditional support.

She'd done the same thing when they'd parted for the last time after graduation. She'd been angry and hurt, but they shared the pain of dismantling the dreams they'd shared through college and law school. Despite the fact that they were causing one another pain, they'd still sought comfort in one another.

When he'd awakened in a medical tent, screaming in pain, it was her touch he'd hallucinated. Hers he'd craved to the point it nearly killed him. He'd endured that long journey back to strength without her.

And now? Now she was the source of the grief and pain, the reason he was in the kitchen while his daughter was one room and a million miles away. Ivy was the one he should be furious with, should be pulling away from.

But her touch was the only comfort that could find its way into his soul. It made no sense.

Did it need to?

She was validating his pain. Acknowledging it existed. That she had played a part in it.

He'd walked through fire without her in Afghanistan. He didn't have to now.

Freeing his hand from her grasp, he turned toward her. His hands found hers again and drew her closer as he rested his forehead against hers. He wanted to tell her it was okay. They could work this out and somehow hold each other up.

He forgave her.

But her breathing shifted. Her fingers tightened in his.

And nothing else mattered. Not betrayal. Not secrets. Not murder.

There was only Ivy, the only one who had ever known the truest parts of him. The only one he'd ever imagined a future with.

In this moment, for the first time in years, that future was close, pulling him in. His lips brushed hers and he hesitated. Did he dare…?

She decided for them both, drawing him out of his hesitation into a kiss the likes of which they'd never shared before.

A fullness expanded in his heart with a feeling he'd never thought he'd experience again. A completion of the man he'd thought he'd lost and could never be again.

He slid his hands up her arms and around her back, drawing her closer. A drowning man who'd been too long without oxygen. A dying man brought back to life.

"I don't know where Mama went." Angie's voice drifted in from the den, too loud, too enthusiastic. It drove a wedge into the space between them.

Ivy jumped back, dragging herself from his arms. She stared at his chest, her fingers pressed to her mouth, her cheeks pink. "Jacob…" She breathed out his name from between her fingers.

Tough to tell if that whisper held recognition or regret. The joy of something she'd lost and found again? Or the grief for something that would remain forever lost?

As little footsteps headed their way, her chin lifted and her brown eyes captured his. She shook her head slightly and turned to face the tiny tornado that tore into the room.

Regret.

Not so for Jacob. Light had come into the darkness. For one brief moment, he'd remembered who he was.

Who he wanted to be again.

"Mama!" Wren launched herself at Ivy, who crouched and met the little girl halfway in a hug. "Come watch *Bross*."

"In a minute, baby." Ivy held her daughter's hands and pivoted on her heels, drawing her around so she stood between them. Whether Wren was a barrier or an offering, Jacob couldn't tell.

Wren looked up at him, her brown eyes serious. "You're Jaycup."

The way she said his name was just about the sweetest sound he'd ever heard. He cleared his throat, trying to control the emotions that rose from being in the presence of both his daughter and his—

And *her* mother. "I am." He crouched to Wren's level, avoiding Ivy's eye. What had just happened was a discussion for another time.

And it would be discussed. Thoroughly. But right now, it was Wren who both demanded and commanded his attention.

"You have bacon." She planted both hands on her hips as if she was accusing him of holding out on her.

Jacob arched an eyebrow and tried not to laugh. "I do." He leaned closer, whispering as though he had a secret. "But I don't have any eggs." He held out both hands to the side and shrugged. "A little bird broke them all."

She giggled, then without warning, threw herself into his arms. "I Wren! I the bird!"

Her laughter slapped his eardrum, and as he tightened his arms for his first hug from his daughter, her warmth and life nearly burst his heart.

Ivy stood and left the room. From the den, he could hear her speaking to Angie, but the only word that landed was *daughter*.

His daughter.

Jacob dipped his head and held the person who had suddenly become the most precious human being in the world close, his eyes and nose stinging from unbidden tears.

He didn't dare flinch or move for fear he'd remind Wren that she preferred to be in motion. He'd seen his daughter in action. She wouldn't hold still for long. But he was going to soak in every ounce of her affection while she offered it.

After a longer time than he'd hoped for and a shorter time than he wanted, she wriggled and backed away. After regarding him with a long look, she tapped the end of his nose. "I boop your nose."

Before he could ask what that meant, she ran away and disappeared into the living room, giggling wildly.

"You're supposed to chase her. It's a game she made up." Ivy stood at the end of the bar that separated the kitchen from the living area, her expression unreadable. She looked down and picked at a fingernail. "She likes you."

In the den, Angie roared like a monster and Wren shrieked.

Jacob stood, his hip protesting the move. He'd almost forgotten what had happened earlier. "I hope she'll more than like me."

Ivy looked up. "We should talk about—"

The shrill ring of his phone stopped her. He'd love to ignore the summons and ask what they needed to discuss. Was it them? That kiss? Wren?

But the gravity of their situation and the threat to her life took precedence over his feelings.

He pulled the phone from his pocket, not recognizing the number, and answered, "Garcia."

"Special Agent Garcia, this is Sheriff Stanton." Jacob exhaled loudly and his stomach clenched. "I'm afraid I have some news."

SEVEN

"Swift River PD wants to talk to Ms. Bridges, and they're going to make that official soon. I'm giving you the courtesy of letting you know." Sheriff Stanton's words practically shook the phone Jacob held to his ear.

Jacob excused himself and stepped out the back door. He walked away from the cabin, just in case his voice carried through the closed windows.

Ivy was preparing to move Wren to the main house, which wasn't in a state of perpetual renovation like the cabin was. It was also a way they could put a bit more distance between them, both physically and emotionally.

It was a necessary move, whether Jacob wanted it or not.

His focus needed to be on protecting Ivy, not on wrestling with how he felt about seeing her again or with how he felt about her hiding Wren from him. "I understand. You have no authority over the police department. It's two separate entities." In the same way Jacob, as a federal agent, had no sway with the county. "I appreciate you standing in the gap for us."

"I trust Chief Davidson. I've known him since he took over the department five years ago. He's not the kind to be involved in corruption or murder. I shared Ivy's state-ment on the Mendez case with him and told him she's safe, but I didn't share where she was. He understood. Still, given that there was a body in her office and that both of our cases have Ms. Bridges at the epicenter, she'll have to come in. There's a lot of tension here, a lot of fear, and people are starting to ask questions."

"But if one of his men tried to kill her, then—"

"He's pretty hot under the collar about that accusa-tion. Isn't sure he believes it." The sheriff exhaled loudly. "Wants to know if she's sure he was a Swift River officer and if she's sure he fired at her and it wasn't just gravel getting kicked up onto her vehicle when she fled."

Jacob's head pounded, his anger rising. Ivy wasn't one to exaggerate or lie. Never had been. But angrily as-serting that to a man who didn't know her wasn't going to help.

She'd parked her car around the back of the cabin the night before, but Jacob hadn't had a chance to inves-tigate the vehicle. Rounding the cabin, Jacob eyed the back of her SUV.

Two bullet holes marred the dark blue liftgate. "Some-one definitely shot at her." He closed the distance and stuck his finger into one of the holes, trying to gauge its size. "I'm no weapons expert, but I don't think it was a small caliber."

The sheriff muttered something under his breath that Jacob probably didn't want to decipher. "What's your honest opinion? Do you really think an officer pulled her over yesterday? Or did she mistake a dark vehicle for a police vehicle?"

"I believe her." Turning away from the SUV, trying not to think about what could have happened to Ivy had she not reacted quickly enough, Jacob faced the woods and chewed the inside of his lower lip. "You still have to take into account she saw a marshal badge at the Mendez home. And she said it was a Swift River cruiser that—"

"Wait. A cruiser?"

"Yes." Jacob froze. Something in the sheriff's voice said there was more to come.

"Not an SUV?"

"No. She's repeatedly said it was a cruiser. Probably the same one I saw leaving her house today. Why?"

"Hmm." The silence stretched so long, Jacob almost believed he could walk it like a tightrope. "SRPD has been phasing out cruisers in favor of SUVs. Last year, they received a sizable grant that let them purchase the SUVs they needed to replace their last two cruisers. Unless I'm remembering wrong, those SUVs were delivered three weeks ago. The cruisers should have gone to be refitted and sent to auction."

"Wait. SRPD has no cruisers currently active?" If Stanton was correct, then that cop wasn't a cop.

And that changed everything.

"I'll call Chief Davidson to be sure, but this could point us in a new direction."

That new direction could lead to the identity of Ivy's attackers. But he couldn't begin to calculate next steps, not yet. Instead, he switched topics. "Is there any word on who was found in her office?" Ivy would ask the instant he went back inside.

The wind kicked up, sending the trees into a brief, frenzied dance. Jacob pressed the phone tighter to his ear and backed into the shelter of the house, watching light and shadow dance in the trees.

"That's another thing I was calling about." Clicks

came through the line as though the sheriff was typing on a keyboard. "I can give you a name."

Jacob's prayer was wordless but crammed with petitions for Ivy not to have to endure any more grief. Although her employees were safe, she still harbored concern for her landlord and others.

As the wind gust eased off, the trees gentled into a rocking motion. Odd, that one quick gust. Reminded him of a poem that had stuck with him since he was a kid.

Who has seen the wind, neither you nor I.

But when the trees bow down their heads, the wind is passing by.

Ever since he'd given his life to Jesus, he'd thought of that little snippet of poetry, how God couldn't be seen but His work could. Times like this, it was nice to think God kind of stirred the trees to remind Jacob that he wasn't by himself.

In the flickering shadows of the trees, something flashed like sunlight on glass, but then it was gone.

Jacob's eyes narrowed. He blinked twice, stepped toward the corner of the cabin and looked again.

Nothing moved except the trees as another gust kicked through, then stilled just as quickly as it rose. He scrubbed his free hand down his cheek and listened to the sheriff type. They probably had an hour before the rain hit, but if the wind was already raging, it wouldn't be pretty when it arrived.

"Got it," the sheriff mumbled as though he was reading something, then his voice raised again. "Guy's name was Anthony Phelps. He's got a record longer than your arm, been picked up for public intoxication and DWI more times than ought to be allowed. Has a couple of assaults and a few B-and-Es to his name, quick hits to garages and sheds to pick up easily pawned items. When he was found this morning, his pockets contained meth, marijuana and a syringe full of enough fentanyl to take out a team of horses."

It was a familiar story, one that never failed to bring sadness. "In any other situation, we'd assume he broke in looking for office equipment or cash." But there was no way it was a coincidence that this guy had died in Ivy's office on the same day she witnessed a murder and was nearly killed herself. Twice.

"Sounds like he wasn't hurting for drugs, given that he had plenty on his person." Including fentanyl. That was messy business. A couple of grains could kill a person. A syringe loaded with the stuff was beyond *a lot.* "Preliminary cause of death?" It could take weeks or months to get back toxicology reports, but the ME would have made an educated guess.

"Strictly preliminary? Overdose. Based on…" More clicks. "Frankly, based on the amount of substances on his person and his physical condition when he was found by Marcie Burns when she showed up to clean the office."

Yeah, the sheriff didn't need to expand any further on the condition of the body. In his short time on the special investigative team, Jacob had seen his share of drug overdoses. They were never pretty. "Thanks, Sheriff. I'll be in touch."

"Hang on." The tone of Sheriff Stanton's voice made Jacob's jaw twitch. "There's a bigger problem."

Hadn't the man already handed him enough trouble for one phone call? This was like falling over the side of the canyon. Uncontrollable, deadly and accelerating by the second. Jacob leaned against the sun-warmed logs on the back side of the cabin, staring at the bullet holes in Ivy's SUV. They needed to dig out the slugs and have them processed. Though it wouldn't be much, they might offer a clue.

But something told him the sheriff's intel needed to come first. "What's wrong?"

"Looking at Phelps's record, there's a list of known associates," Stanton said. "One of them is Sienna Davies."

"What?" A sudden shot of adrenaline shoved Jacob away from the house and sent him pacing for the woods. "Sienna Davies? You're sure?"

"'Fraid so."

Born and raised in Wales, Davies had made the move to Nevada a dozen or more years prior. She'd started as muscle for small-time gamblers and had moved up until she'd made a name for herself as a killer for hire, suspected in a dozen murders across the Southwest over the last decade, mostly people who crossed local gangs or tried to move in on their territory.

But a few months earlier, her calling card had been connected to a hit on a Nevada state senate candidate. The upstart politician, Dustin Aguilar, was found drowned in his swimming pool. A two-dollar bill was anchored beneath a candle on a nearby picnic table.

Rumor had it he'd taken contributions from the wrong people and had failed to deliver on promises made to them, though no concrete evidence of wrongdoing by Aguilar was ever found.

But Sienna Davies was moving up in the world.

"That has to be a coincidence. Maybe they crossed paths once." Jacob's gut twisted, quick to remind him *coincidence* rarely existed in his line of work.

"Anything is possible, but..."

But a lethal syringe of fentanyl in the pocket of a

known associate of Davies, one found dead in Ivy's office? That wasn't random. "Tell me that Phelps didn't have a two-dollar bill on him."

"Other than the drugs, I don't have an itemized list, but I'll find out. I'm sure SRPD has already made the connection and is checking, but I'll alert Chief Davidson just in case they missed it. If they find Davies's calling card, it's going to change the scope of this entire investigation."

It would escalate things quickly, that was certain. "Update me when you can. And thanks for your help." Jacob ended the call and shoved his phone into his back pocket.

The breeze had completely died, following its usual random spring pattern. But based on the clouds piling up in the distance, it would pick up again with no shortage of ferocity.

He glanced at his watch. Linc needed to get here with those files and with his considerable amount of experience and wisdom. It was one thing to protect Ivy from amateurs. Jacob felt confident he could handle that.

But if a killer on the level of Sienna Davies was behind this, there was much more at stake. There was no—

His peripheral vision picked up movement.

Whipping toward the woods, Jacob scanned the trees. Either there had been another flash of light, or his eyes were playing tricks on him.

It wouldn't hurt to check. Forcing himself to keep his hand away from the semiautomatic at his side, Jacob strode toward the woods. It wouldn't do to scare off one of the guest scientists at the ranch who'd hiked away from the main camp and stumbled on his cabin.

When he was about twenty yards from the tree line, something crashed and bolted deeper into the trees.

Breaking into a run, Jacob gave chase, not caring any

longer if the perpetrator was a ranch guest. Ivy's life was at stake.

About ten yards in, he stopped and listened, but nothing moved. Nothing looked suspicious. Just a few crushed leaves and twigs where something big had moved through.

He scanned the area one more time and headed back to the cabin, glancing back more than once, feeling as though he was being watched.

It could have been an animal. A wandering researcher.

Or something much more deadly.

She had lost control of her life.

Ivy bounced in the seat as Jacob's pickup hit a rut in the long dirt road that wove between stands of trees and open country on the way to the main ranch house. In the near distance, a ravine ran parallel to the property and opened up into the Grand Canyon, various cliffs and spaces falling into deeper shadows as the clouds thickened.

Another jolt was enough to jar her fingers away from her lips, where she could still feel Jacob's kiss.

Or had she kissed him? In the end, it didn't matter who started it. They'd kissed.

More than that, they'd complicated everything even more.

There was no way this was her life. Jacob… Contract killers… Maybe she was living in a nightmare.

On the bench seat between them, Wren wriggled in her car seat. This journey was an adventure for the innocent little girl. Every moment was a carnival of new sights, sounds and faces.

"You okay over there?" For the first time since they'd loaded the truck, Jacob spoke.

Something was on his mind, and it was more than their kiss. When he'd walked into the cabin earlier, his face had been hard-edged and his complexion tinged red.

He'd given Ivy a brief rundown of his call with the sheriff. The SRPD officer was an impersonator, but there was no word on the federal agent who'd attacked her.

Worse, she might be in the crosshairs of a rifle aimed by Sienna Davies. Even Ivy recognized that name, and she'd never expected to be linked to the woman.

Jacob had also announced a change of plans. He was relocating with them. He'd dropped a duffel bag into the bed of the truck beside her backpack and Wren's day care bag.

"Ivy? I asked if you're okay."

Not trusting herself to speak, Ivy nodded. Too much was happening at once. Her heart and her mind spun too violently for her to grasp one.

She was running for her life and Wren's.

She'd kissed Jacob.

Repeat.

As the sun edged closer to the horizon, she braced her elbow on the door and planted her palm against her cheek, letting her head rock with each dip in the farm road that led from the cabin to the main house. Weary from fighting the storm, she gave in and let it carry her, like Dorothy transported to a strange Oz populated with familiar faces.

How many times had she sat in this very seat and ridden up this very road with this very man at her side? How many times had she dreamed of the day when they'd make this trip with their child between them?

Oh, my word, she was going to be sick.

Ivy dug her fingers into her scalp and bit her lower lip, wrestling exhaustion, fear and guilt.

So much guilt over deciding for Jacob that he wouldn't want to be tied down to a wife and a child he'd never asked for.

If only she'd given him the choice from the start.

She'd seen his face when Wren dove into his arms. Pain. Peace.

Love.

In that moment, the ramifications of her decisions had slapped her. She'd been wrong.

She dared to glance over Wren's head at him. How did he feel knowing he'd missed the joy of anticipation and the feeling of baby kicks against a waiting hand? That he'd been denied first laughs? First steps?

For four years, she'd been certain she'd made the right decision for him.

For him. She had no right to make any decision *for him.*

Jesus, now what? Jacob was supposed to be happy somewhere out there without us. He was never supposed to come back. It wasn't part of the plan.

Neither was kissing him. But she had. And in spite of her situation and the danger, being in his arms had unlocked feelings she'd been denying for years.

She'd never fully released Jacob, and that had nothing to do with Wren.

It had everything to do with being half of a person without him.

"Seriously, you're too quiet." Jacob's low voice floated to her again, punctuated by another giggle from Wren as the truck jarred in another rut.

"There's a lot to deal with."

Truer words had never been spoken.

His jaw worked forward and back. He was chewing the inside of his lip again. It was a familiar gesture. Was he thinking about that kiss? Or had he dismissed it? "You've been through a lot the past couple of days."

A metal cattle guard, a remnant from the pre-retreat days when the land had been a working cattle ranch, rattled beneath the tires as he slowed the truck near the house.

"You have no idea." She muttered the words then turned toward her daughter. *Their* daughter. The daughter she'd brought to Jacob because she could trust no one else to protect them.

There was that word again. *Trust.* In spite of the years between them and the way he'd walked away from their dreams, she trusted him with her life. With their daughter's life.

When Jacob pulled around the circular drive in front of the house and shifted the truck into Park, Ivy leaned forward for a better look.

Although his father had passed and his mother had moved to live with her sister, nothing had changed about the Garcia home in the years since she'd been welcomed like family. The white brick house with cedar trim sprawled across the landscape. Jacob's great-grandfather had built a smaller house when he moved out of the original cabin. Over the years, the family had added on as needed. Although it was large, the house was comfortable and welcoming.

The same well-kept landscaping framed the front of the house. The same steps led to the same wide front porch. The familiar row of wooden rocking chairs waited for sweet tea and conversation.

Or hand-holding and dreams of the future in the softness of a summer night.

Ivy clamped down on the memories. Even though Jacob was back, he still had a job that could require him to move at the whim of the government. That could see him walk out the door one morning and never return.

How would that affect Wren? Constant military moves during her childhood had left Ivy bitter. And her father's death when she was a teenager had gutted her. Wren deserved stability and a life without constant fear.

As much as Ivy had tried to construct a safe life for her daughter, fear had still found her.

Ivy let her seat belt run through her fingers, then twisted to unbuckle Wren, pasting on a smile. "You ready to see where we're going to stay?"

"Horse!" Wren clapped her hands and pointed past the house to the barn that stood nearby, nearly taking out Ivy's left eye in her enthusiasm.

"Yes." Jacob unbuckled his seat belt, but he didn't look at Wren. Instead, he leaned forward and seemed to be searching for something between the house and the horse barn. "That's the house."

Why was he so distracted? "She said *horse*."

"What?" He glanced at her, his jaw tight. He looked past her out the side window, then twisted in the seat to look out the back window of the truck.

He wasn't just distracted. He was brooding.

Turning her attention back to Wren, Ivy hefted her out of the car seat and into her lap for a better view.

Wren pounded the window with her palms, leaving tiny handprints behind. "Horses, Mama!"

Ivy managed to catch Jacob's eye and halt his restless searching. "She sees the horses in the corral by the barn."

A light sparked in Jacob's eye, and he seemed to relax. At least he stopped scanning the area like he expected an armed assault. He sat back against the door and addressed Wren. "Horses are a lot of fun, but you have to be careful, too."

Already, he was parenting. Far from being awkward, it was comforting.

Ivy studied him as he pointed at and named the horses. He'd changed into jeans and his black work jacket, the one he often wore around the ranch. He was the same cowboy who'd stolen her heart when he walked into the cafeteria on the first day of classes their freshman year, dark from the sun and in full swagger.

When he turned, he caught Ivy staring and a slight smile lifted his mouth. "So, are we shocked the kid loves horses?" Having completely shed his earlier tension, Jacob lifted a dark eyebrow in question, that smile hinting that he might know what Ivy was thinking.

And that couldn't happen. No matter how much her heart pulled her toward Jacob, the same obstacles that had driven them apart five years earlier stood between them now. Clearing her throat, Ivy turned her attention to Wren and pointed to the porch. "Look, Wren. On the porch."

Ever the show-off, Wren arched her back and shouted, "We rock!" Her mouth stayed wide open as she locked her dark eyes on Jacob. "Mama and me rock."

Jacob's smile shifted from genuine to a pasted-on facade, almost as though he could sense that Ivy was using Wren as a buffer. "You certainly do rock."

Ivy ignored his tone and held Wren's waist, bouncing

her daughter gently. "Wren loves a good rocking chair, don't you, jelly bean?"

Giggling, Wren exaggerated her up-and-down motion, nearly touching the roof of the truck with her head.

With a chuckle that sounded forced, Jacob turned and opened the truck door.

But before he could get out of the pickup, Wren stopped bouncing and made a leap toward the driver's seat. "Jaycup!"

Only Ivy's quick reflexes caught her daughter before she tumbled headlong over her car seat. She released Wren slowly so she could scramble across the seat, where she launched into Jacob's arms.

Wren rarely wanted anyone's attention before she knew them well. She tended to cling to Ivy when strangers were near.

Maybe, on some deeper level, she knew exactly who the man she called "Jaycup" really was.

Jacob snuggled Wren close. "Let's go see those horses." His voice was husky, straight from the heart. She'd heard that timbre before.

When he was breaking her heart.

She slid out of the truck and followed as father and daughter walked and chattered. The gusty wind from earlier raised into a steady breeze, bringing the scent of distant rain.

As they neared the corral, Ivy watched the horses. One in particular, a dusty, palomino quarter horse, caught her attention. Was that Jacob's horse? Shiloh? How was it even possible that Shiloh was still...?

Motion drew her attention away from the horse. At the back corner of the barn, a man in a dark jacket eased out of the shadows. When he spotted Ivy, he ducked back into shelter.

Ivy blinked slowly. Had she seen that? Or was her exhausted mind finally giving way?

"Mama. Move." Wren waved at her over Jacob's shoulder, but Ivy's feet were rooted to the ground.

Jacob must have sensed she was no longer with them. He turned, shielding Wren from the wind with his body. "What's wrong?"

Jacob's low tone jolted her into exhaling the breath she'd been holding. "Do you guys still have ranch hands?"

"We let them go when we let the cattle go, after Dad died. There's a few head of cattle down near the guest cabins, but they belong to the conservation group. They're doing sustainability research. Why?"

"I just..." She shook her head to clear it. This was silly. She was seeing things after the exhaustion and chaos of the last couple of days. "It's nothing. I just thought I saw somebody behind the barn."

Jacob strode over and passed Wren to her. "Get in the house. Now." Without watching to see if she obeyed, he ran past her and headed for the barn, his hand already on his pistol.

EIGHT

Thunder rumbled across the landscape, that strange, echo-filled thunder that only happened in close proximity to the canyon. It seemed to mimic the whomping of Jacob's heart as he rounded the corner of the big white barn.

He tried to still a rising paranoia. Probably, a researcher had wandered too far from the research facility.

Or perhaps someone had found Ivy here, where she should have been safe.

The first drops of wind-driven rain stung his cheeks as he searched the area behind the barn. The wind howled around the building, whipping a loose tarp over another of his father's old pickups where it waited beneath a lean-to to be restored.

Creeping along the back of the barn, Jacob tried to shelter himself from the rain and wind, but it was futile. The cold front unleashed its full fury, and the deluge immediately soaked his clothing. He gave up trying to stay dry and focused on the search.

Already, the rain had drenched the ground enough that any footprints were obliterated.

He peered in the window of the old office, but it was empty. The back door that led to the office and storage area was locked. And the huge sliding doors that led to the main horse barn were firmly shut and padlocked. Angie had probably left them closed, knowing that storms were likely.

At the lean-to, he peeked under the tarp and checked the truck bed before securing the bungee cord that had come loose and left the tarp flapping.

He finally relaxed and gave in to the soaking rain. There was no one there.

But surely Ivy wasn't imagining things?

If she was as exhausted as he was, then a shift of the light as the wind kicked up looked like—

Yeah, even *his* sometimes overactive imagination wasn't *that* good.

Lightning struck a stand of firs between the main house and the cabin, thunder following instantly. He should get inside before the storm permanently kept him from having to worry about contract killers ever again.

After sliding open the back barn doors, he slipped into the warmth of the interior and shut the doors behind him. The cold front had already dropped the temperature about ten degrees, and it was still plummeting. Tonight would be frigid. They'd have to make sure to run the heat in the barn to keep the horses warm if it fell as far as Angie had hinted it might.

Having a meteorologist for a sister was a blessing.

He shook the excess water off his baseball cap then swiped his arms down his coat, grateful it had shed most of the water.

The familiar scents of horse and hay enveloped him as their four horses wandered in from the corral, seeking shelter from the storm. Might as well secure them.

Either Angie or he could come out later and bed them down for the night.

Like the well-trained animals they were, each horse made its way to his own stall, searching for warmth in the diving temperatures.

Jacob strode along the barn's center aisle, peeking into stalls and checking in storage rooms, just in case someone had made their way inside. He secured each stall behind him, scratching the horses on their noses with a promise of dinner as soon as the clock cycled to their usual five-thirty feeding time.

Angie would have his head if he knocked them off their schedule by feeding them now.

When he finished, he doubled back to the rear stall on the left.

Shiloh hung her head over the door to watch him.

Resting his forehead against hers, Jacob patted her long neck. She'd been with him since he started high school, and although she was getting "long in the tooth," she still loved a good run across the ranch and along the ravine.

"As soon as Ivy and Wren are safe, it's me and you, girl. A whole day." He'd been neglecting her while his team hunted Daniel Adams and his well-coordinated ring of artifact smugglers in the canyon. With all of the revelations and dangers that had rained down on him in the last twenty-four hours, he was aching for a wide-open haul to the rim. "We could both use the exercise, huh, girl?"

She nickered softly, almost as though she understood him, and shoved her nose into his chest with enough force to knock him back a step.

He chuckled and gave her a final scratch between her huge brown eyes. "I get it. You agree."

Not too far off, the rumble of an engine filtered through the pounding of rain on the metal roof. Sounded like Linc had arrived.

At the door, Jacob peered out into the deluge as Linc parked the truck next to Jacob's old Ford. Finally, maybe they'd have some answers.

Before Jacob could run across the corral to the house a short distance away, Linc spotted him and jogged over, trying unsuccessfully to keep his head dry under the hood of his rain jacket. He tore into the barn with an audible *brrrr* and a shiver, shaking off the rain. "That storm is wild." He shucked back his hood and scrubbed water from his dark blond hair. "Don't know why I even bothered with the jacket."

"It should end quick. It's a line of storms with a cold front. Temps will be brutal tonight, though."

Linc stopped scrubbing at his head and lifted his gaze, his head still tilted down. "You've been talking to your sister."

Jacob shrugged and let that comment go. Whatever had happened between Angie and Linc while Jacob was recovering had remained between the two of them. They'd never said anything to him, but it was clear by the way they avoided each other that something had occurred to mar the friendship they'd once enjoyed.

One of them would talk eventually. Until they did, Jacob would keep his observations to himself. "Did you have any trouble?"

"Nope."

"Backpack's in your truck?"

"I figured dragging it out in the rain wasn't the smartest move. We'll grab it when this lets up." Linc leaned against a closed storage-room door near the entrance and crossed his arms, eyeing Jacob. "So you want to tell me what's got you all spun up? Besides Ivy?"

"I—" Jacob shut his mouth and turned to stare out at the rain. He'd expected questions, but not so soon. "Nothing."

"Uh-huh." Linc's voice held a familiar half laugh. It was the same tone Jacob had heard a hundred times overseas, when Linc was somewhere between amused at a subordinate's behavior and highly annoyed at the same time. "You were not yourself today. Nearly got all three of us killed."

"You could have chimed in and pulled rank or something."

"This isn't a mission, and I'm not calling the shots." Linc knocked his knuckles against the door behind him, a rhythmic tap that crawled all over Jacob's already fraying nerves. "And don't try to deflect the blame toward me for anything that happened today."

He was right, of course. Linc had always been the thinker and the planner, while Jacob had proven more likely to run into situations first and ask questions later. He'd been a good soldier, but he'd barely scraped out with his life a few times when he'd let his adrenaline get ahead of his common sense.

Ironic that the time he *wasn't* charging ahead was the time he'd lost everything.

He sniffed and walked toward the huge open barn entrance, leaning against the door that mirrored the one Linc had lounged against. Shoving his hands into his coat pockets, he stretched out his legs and stared at his boots. It was harder to say than he'd imagined, and this would be the first time the words left his lips. It felt like there should be fireworks or a rifle salute or something. "It's not just Ivy."

"Okay."

"I mean, it's partially her. I'm figuring out fast that some feelings never died." That kiss in the kitchen today had proven it. His heart had responded to her as though they'd never been apart, as though she hadn't betrayed him and denied him the chance to know his daughter for the last four years.

"You're the only one who didn't already know that." Linc stopped knocking on the door and shoved his hands into his pockets, his posture mimicking Jacob's. "All you talked about from the moment I met you was Ivy. I doubt you realized how much she peppered your words. Your entire squad—no, make that half of the company—knew her favorite food and song and movie within the first week of deployment. By the time you headed back stateside, we all felt like we knew her. There was practically a big-brother style protection of her happening." He chuckled. "And a whole lot of the guys took her side. Thought you were a total idiot for not fighting for her when you signed on the dotted line."

"I wasn't going to do that." Ivy's past was marred with pain. He'd never wanted to add to that.

"You weren't? Because you didn't want to hurt her? Or because you were afraid no amount of fighting would ever make you more important to her than her fear was?"

The words almost knocked Jacob backward. If he hadn't been leaning against the door, he'd have probably landed on his rear on the dusty floor. He balled his fists in the pockets of his coat, ready to argue.

No, actually ready to fight.

Except something he'd recognized as a nudge from

God turned his thoughts. He stared at his toes, digging his teeth into the inside of his bottom lip. Was that it? Was his entire high-and-mighty sacrifice of their relationship more about being afraid of rejection than it was about protecting her?

Those were bigger thoughts than he could consider right now. Instead, he kicked the dirt at his feet, then looked up at Linc. "Her daughter, Wren, is—is my daughter."

Not even a flicker of surprise tweaked Linc's features. He watched Jacob for a long moment, then the right side of his mouth tilted slightly. "I figured. I just wanted to hear you say it. You needed to be the one to put it out there. To own that you're a father."

Jacob nodded slowly, Linc's words echoing his earlier thoughts. "How did you know?"

"The kid's four years old. You signed up five years ago. Doesn't take a math genius." Linc let loose with a full-on grin. "Congrats, brother. I know what this has to mean to you, given..." His smile slipped. Few people knew that the IED had wreaked havoc on Jacob's internal organs as severely as they had. But Linc did.

Jacob didn't respond. Why should he, when Linc already seemed to know everything?

"Listen." Straightening, his former squad leader and current team leader pushed away from the door and strode across the aisle, resting a hand on Jacob's shoulder as though he was decades older instead of only a couple of years Jacob's senior. "It's going to take some time for you to sort this all out, and you don't need to do it today. There are more immediate concerns. But if you can't get your head in the game and stop thinking with your emotions and your reactions instead of your responses, then you need to hand over Ivy and Wren's protection to someone else. I get you want answers, but you can't keep making dangerous calls like you did today."

He was right, whether Jacob liked it or not.

After squeezing Jacob's shoulder one last time, Linc backed away. "Rain's slacked up. Let's get that backpack and go see if we can find the answers you need."

"Before we go inside..." Jacob waited for Linc to stop walking. "There's more." Like this attack was coordinated and planned. And one of the most notorious contract killers in the southwest had Ivy in her sights.

Finally dressed in her own clothes from the backpack Linc had delivered, Ivy slid into a chair at the huge plankwood dining-room table and dropped the Mendez estate file next to the laptop Angie had loaned her.

She planted both hands on the thick file, resting her palms on the card stock as she closed her eyes. *Lord, we need answers. We need to know who killed Clarissa, who's chasing me, who threatened Wren. Please.* She let the stillness around her settle onto her skin, resting in the sense of God's presence and in the warmth that she remembered from so many family meals shared in this room.

Ivy let herself relax into a sense of safety. At this moment, in this room, no one was aiming a gun at her or even drawing back to toss a Molotov cocktail through the window.

Jacob had passed her the backpack and suggested she change, then he'd jogged up the stairs to get into dry clothes after his search outside.

When the rain stopped, Angie had loaded Wren into the pickup to go back to the cabin, where Wren had left her stuffed bunny. They planned to ride over to the conservation land to look at the cattle there so that Ivy would have time to read through the file without interruption.

At Ivy's request, Linc had gone with them. They might be safe on the ranch, but she felt a lot better with an armed federal agent along for the ride. However, she hadn't missed the awkward greeting between Jacob's sister and his closest friend. Something hovered between them. In a different time, she'd have dragged Angie aside and told her to spill it.

But that really was a different time. Before an assassin had targeted her.

Before she'd hidden Wren from her father.

Ivy's chin sank to her chest. It didn't matter that her old feelings for Jacob weren't old and never had been. Everything revolved around Wren and what she needed.

Could she wrestle down her fear and build the life she'd never truly stopped dreaming about with Jacob?

Would he even want to try after she'd betrayed him so arrogantly?

She balled her hands into fists on top of the folder. *And, Lord, please. This thing with Jacob and Wren is a tangled mess. My heart is a tangled mess. I want—*

"You ready?" Jacob's deep voice fell over her prayer like a warm blanket.

Like the voice she wanted to hear for the rest of her life.

The thought jolted her, and her head jerked up, her hands falling into her lap.

"Sorry. Didn't mean to scare you." Jacob pulled out the chair beside hers and sat, clueless that his sudden appearance hadn't been what startled her. Just his presence had shot that lightning bolt through her.

And it had put the brakes on a request she wasn't certain she should be praying.

"It's okay." Ivy breathed deeply and exhaled slowly, trying to ignore that Jacob's knee brushed hers under the table and that she could feel the warmth of him from where he sat.

"You ready?" He'd changed into jeans and a sage-green sweater and looked entirely more relaxed than she felt. "Let's do this."

But she didn't move. She just sat with her hands in her lap, her fingers twined together, staring at the folder.

"Ives?" It was the second time he'd called her by the nickname that only he called her, the one she'd cherished above all others. "You okay?"

She nodded jerkily, then tilted her head to look him in the eye, dragging her attention out of her private feelings and into the moment that might save her life…or destroy it. "What if there are no answers?" It was her darkest fear, eclipsing even the fear of losing Jacob if she allowed herself to love him again.

"Only one way to find out."

"But what if I risked your life to retrieve a folder that's just a run-of-the-mill estate and a bunch of worthless old stocks and bonds? What if we're no closer to the end?" She picked up the folder, gripping it so hard it nearly bent in her hands. "What if this doesn't tell us anything? Doesn't stop this?" Her voice shook. For the first time, it hit her that the rest of her life could be spent on the run, in hiding, dragging Wren from place to place.

Just like the army had dragged her family all over the country until her father's death.

Jacob's expression softened into sympathy. Gently, he pulled the file from her grip and laid it on the table, then wrapped his fingers around hers. "Then we'll get through this together."

How was she supposed to respond to that? *Together* could mean a lot of different things. And when it came to Jacob, *together* there were too many complications.

Extracting her fingers from his grasp, Ivy reached for the folder again.

"I need to tell you something first. I didn't want to talk about it in front of Wren."

No. They couldn't have a relationship conversation now, not when her life was in chaos and she had no idea how her heart felt. But the expression on his face wasn't one of hope or longing. It was more serious, more concerned.

That phone call with the sheriff had yielded information. Her throat went dry, and all of her questions lodged in the desert.

"They identified the man in your office. He was a known drug user and petty criminal with no known connection to you."

Exhaling a breath she hadn't realized she'd been holding, she slouched in the seat. Immediately, guilt replaced her relief. While it might not be someone close to her, a man was still dead. A family would still grieve. That was a tragedy. "How did he die?"

"They're waiting on the full autopsy and on toxicology." He looked away, and his finger tapped a slow drumbeat on the table. It was the same tic he always had when there was something difficult to discuss.

"What else?" Because there had to be more if he was acting like this.

He glanced at her then turned fully to face her, clasping his hands on the table in front of him. His movement flowed, professional and practiced, probably something he'd picked on the job. He was shifting gears, moving into work mode and out of the personal realm. "Swift River PD no longer utilizes cruisers. Their entire working fleet was converted to SUVs."

Crossing her arms on her stomach, Ivy stared at the gleaming stainless-steel refrigerator in the kitchen. The surface was covered with magnets and notes, as jumbled as her mind. But one of the memories snagged on something and held firm. "I think I remember something about that being news around town, but I didn't realize…" She dug her fingers into her arms, relief almost sliding her to the floor. "So it wasn't a police officer who shot at me?"

"We can't rule that out entirely, but it's looking like someone got their hands on a cruiser that was supposed to be refitted or they bought an old one and repainted it. Sheriff Stanton is going to get with the chief and see if they can track down their recycled vehicles."

"But why? That's a lot of trouble to go to for Clarissa Mendez. Or for me." And why did the man at Mr. Mendez's house have a federal badge? This was more than a random act or a last-minute murder. It was coordinated. Planned.

And she'd landed in the cross fire.

A wave of dizziness struck, and she grabbed the edge of the table to stabilize herself. Somehow, knowing the man might have gone to great lengths to impersonate an officer made everything worse. "Is there anything else?"

Jacob hesitated, his grip on his fingers tightening until his knuckles turned white. "No."

He wasn't telling her the truth. The answer was too clipped.

She started to call him on it, then stopped. At the moment, she didn't want to dive into his reasoning. She just wanted answers. To make it stop.

Ivy took another deep breath and flipped open the folder. On top was the large envelope Clarissa had handed her a few days ago that contained stocks and bonds she'd found taped to the bottom of a drawer on her uncle's desk at the shop.

This could give them the answers. If there were stocks worth millions, then they might have a start at discovering motive.

Undoing the clasp, she slid the papers onto the table. Some of them were yellow with age. She paged through carefully, passing the stock certificates to Jacob one by one as she read them. "I don't recognize any of these companies."

Jacob opened the laptop and started typing. "It'll take a lot more digging to be sure, but..." He flipped through a few of the pages, typing as he did. "Most of these companies don't exist anymore. I mean, they could have merged with others, but none of these appear to be worth a great deal. At least not enough to—" He fell silent.

To kill for.

He cleared his throat. "There are stocks that can be valuable simply because they're collectible, but that doesn't appear to be the case with any of these." Sliding the stack to the other side of the laptop, he looked up at Ivy, his expression grave. "This isn't it."

She'd so wanted it to be *it*. She stopped sifting through the bonds she'd been scanning. "Let's face it. Even if they were worth millions somehow, all that would give us is motive. There'd be nothing to point us in the direction of specific people."

"True." Jacob tilted his head toward the papers she was holding. "Anything in the bonds?"

"No." She dropped the stack onto the left side of the folder. "They all reached maturity years ago, so they stopped earning interest. And they're all small amounts. Altogether, there's a couple thousand dollars, maybe."

Bracing her elbow on the table, she propped her forehead against her palm. "I just don't know." Someone had leaked all of the air from her hope. Her spirits sank like a hot-air balloon with the heat turned off.

And they hadn't been flying that high to begin with.

"Okay." Jacob sat up and slid the computer into the center of the table. "We were guessing it might be about money. Maybe there's something else." He jerked his head toward the folder. "What else is in that file?"

"A will. Standard. Nothing out of the ordinary. He'd already signed over the shop and his assets to Clarissa, so the only thing left was the house, which also went to her. And if she preceded him in death, then it went to the foster-care advocacy group in town. That's where it will go now, since—"

"Something on the property then?" He sat straighter, as though he was getting excited. "Maybe somebody is trying to force a sale. Mineral rights? Oil? Natural gas?"

"Possibly. But I think he left instructions to have the house used as a home for children aging out of the system, sort of a jumping-off place. His heart was with Clarissa when her parents passed away." Ivy reached for the will to make sure. "If he hadn't been able to take her in, she'd have gone into—"

A thick white envelope, caught on the staple that held

the will together, slipped from the folder and landed in Ivy's lap.

She stared at it, afraid to touch it. She hadn't put that in the file. Had never seen it before.

Her heart rate tripled. This. This could be their answer.

NINE

Jacob shoved the chair away from the table and stood, ready to do battle.

But there was nothing to fight. There was only an envelope, resting in Ivy's lap. Whatever it contained, it had stopped her cold. "Ivy, what's wrong?"

She was silent. In the stillness that fell between them, he could hear the horses whinnying in the barn, probably protesting the change in air pressure brought on by the earlier storm.

"I don't recognize this." Gingerly, between two fingers, she lifted the envelope and settled it on the table between them, almost as if it burned.

Or as if she thought it might vanish into dust if she handled it too roughly.

Jacob slid his chair closer to the table and sat, eyeing the plain white business envelope. It looked too nondescript to be holding possible life-saving information. Still… "This could be what they're looking for."

"Or it could be more worthless stocks. Regardless, Clarissa must have put it in the file when she brought the bonds over to the office. It was on my desk, and I left the room for a few minutes while she was there to make some copies." She shoved it closer to Jacob. "You open it."

He did, surprised to find his own hand shook slightly. Adrenaline. Somehow, he just knew…this was the key to ending the threat to Ivy's life.

He dumped out the contents of the envelope. There were about ten sheets of paper, folded in thirds. Some had been typed on a computer while others were handwritten on plain notebook paper. "Looks like letters." He passed them to Ivy, not quite clear on what he legally could and couldn't observe in her files. The last thing he wanted to do now was cross any legal lines.

She scanned the pages then sat straighter, her hope returning. "Jacob…" Her voice shook. When she finished scanning the first page, she looked up. "This can't be real."

"What?" Her face had gone pale, and she held the letters as though she was afraid someone would snatch them from their hands.

"These aren't exactly letters. They're more like journal entries and notes. Mr. Mendez was not Edward Mendez. He was Patrick Ramirez. Born in Tucson. And according to this he kept the books for a big-time loan shark in Las Vegas back in the late nineties, then testified against the guy in return for immunity. These are all things he wrote down. Stories. Bank-account numbers. Eyewitness accounts."

"So either he ran and changed his name or WITSEC was involved." It wasn't such a far-fetched idea. Organized crime was woven through Las Vegas's history. Although the city had become much more family- and tourist-friendly over the years, there were still threads of corruption and criminal activity. There was a long list of people who had traded their identities for immunity and freedom.

"If these are to be believed, then yes, although he didn't move very far out of town. And apparently he also took several million dollars of the organization's money with him when he got out."

"Somebody wants that money back." And Ivy was likely holding the key to where it was hidden.

She looked up from the letters. "I don't understand. He was the nicest man. Kind and generous. How could he also be...?" She shook her head. "I just can't picture him running with the mob."

"People change. Sounds like he did." So where had he hidden the money? "You think Clarissa found those letters and slipped them in your file? Maybe she thought she was in danger and was trying to preserve the evidence? It could be she hid them expecting to retrieve them later."

"That would explain why she trusted the man with the marshal badge and why they chose to approach her as law enforcement. If they suspected she knew, it would make sense to approach her as a federal investigator or as a cop. They could point to his past." She flipped to the next page and read, then muttered to herself, "But why wait until he was dead?"

It was possible they'd murdered him and then had to go after Clarissa as well. If Clarissa had told them she'd handed off the paperwork to Ivy, then that explained their desire to get to her and her files. But there was no closure until they could figure out exactly who it was that wanted that money. "How did he pass away?"

"Hmm?" Ivy looked up from reading. "Oh. He was a heavy smoker. He had lung cancer."

"There was an obituary? Online? In the papers?" It

was a long shot, but it was possible that had been the thing to tip off his former colleagues to his whereabouts.

"The local news did a story on him and his work with the foster…" Ivy sucked in a sharp breath. "Jacob. If anyone who was looking for the missing money saw that story…"

Then they'd found a treasure map.

Only one thing didn't make sense. Clarissa had been raised by Edward Mendez. The entire estate went to her. Sure, there might be a paper trail in those notes, but there was no guarantee. And if anyone would know where the money was, it would be Clarissa. Why would someone murder her before they had the cash in hand?

Jacob rocked the chair onto its back legs and stared at the ceiling. They were missing something. It just didn't add up.

Ivy had been threatened at the murder scene. She'd found Clarissa's body. But she hadn't seen the murder happen. She hadn't even seen the killer until he intentionally came after her.

Killing her to keep her silent as a witness would be a spur-of-the-moment crime of passion. But the man who'd attempted to murder her knew who she was. He knew she had a daughter and had threatened Wren by name.

They'd researched Ivy, had possibly been watching her for some time. And that made zero sense if this was all about hidden money.

No. There was more. People were hunted and silenced because of something they *knew*, not because of something they *had*.

As if they could feel his agitation from a distance, the horses whinnied again.

Jacob couldn't make two and two equal four. His chair

thunked to the floor as he sat forward. "Who was the loan shark?"

"Gabriel Simmons." Ivy kept reading. "It says here he managed to evade prosecution for years because he was protected by…" She lowered the papers slowly, her jaw slack.

"By who?" Jacob reached for the paper and gently pulled it from Ivy's hand, then scanned the page. These notes were thorough, listing names and dates, even banks and safe-deposit box numbers. Maybe it wasn't about the money. Maybe the information in these notes was what Sienna Davies and her goons had been hired to protect.

"Gabriel Simmons," Jacob murmured as he read. He'd studied that case in college, fascinated by all of the moving parts that had kept Simmons above the law for years…and how that house of cards came falling down. He'd been untouchable until an informant turned on him—likely Edward Mendez. Simmons had gone down with his entire organization, so there was no one left in his crew to come after these papers.

That meant someone else wanted their involvement kept under wraps.

In order to avoid prosecution, Simmons would have needed inside help, someone in the government. But no officials had ever been indicted, even though several were investigated. Still, someone had kept him clean.

Someone like… His gaze landed on the name. A district court judge named Ross Evans.

The paper detailed bribes and bank accounts, cases and evidence linked to Evans. While the unauthenticated letter likely wouldn't hold up in court, it was a treasure map to hard evidence that Edward Mendez had tucked away.

Evidence that could land Ross Evans in very deep, very hot water.

"Evans is a state representative now, right?" Jacob scanned the pages, noting bank names where Mendez was holding safe-deposit boxes.

"For now." Ivy got up and walked into the kitchen. She pulled a bottle of water from the fridge and leaned against the door. "He's running for an open senate seat, has his eyes on Washington."

Two plus two equals four. Jacob stood, reaching for his phone. This was the thing someone was willing to kill for. Ross Evans had been running against Dustin Aguilar, the politician who was found dead in his swimming pool with Sienna Davies's calling card nearby. "If this got out, it would wreck Evans's senate run and would almost certainly land him in jail. A clear link between Evans and organized crime would drive his life straight off a cliff."

"It would also call into question every case he ever presided over as a judge." Ivy walked back into the dining area, the water bottle shaking slightly in her hand. "This is definitely enough for a man to think he has to kill for."

It also explained why Ivy was on the hit list. Ross Evans had no idea who had actually seen those files. He'd likely handed over a list of everyone who had access to Edward Mendez's records. As the Mendez attorney, Ivy would be a logical target as a possible confidante.

Clarissa had been target number one. Under duress, she'd likely confess that she'd slipped the information into Ivy's files, making Ivy a clear target number two.

Given that Anthony Phelps had been found in Ivy's office with enough fentanyl to slaughter a platoon of soldiers... His connection to Sienna Davies made it highly likely that she was the killer behind Clarissa's murder and the attempt on Ivy's life.

She'd sent her lackeys to do what she viewed to be an easy job.

A professional like Sienna Davies wouldn't make that mistake again.

Ivy paced from the table to the window and back. "What do we do now?"

"We don't sit on the evidence, that's for sure." Spreading the pages out on the table, Jacob started snapping photos. "I'm calling Sheriff Stanton and a buddy of mine who works for the FBI." When Ivy started to protest, he looked up from his phone. "I trust him."

"I don't know." She puffed out her cheeks and walked to the window again, exhaling loudly. After stopping halfway, she turned back. "That Phelps guy, from my office. Do you have a photo of him?"

"I'm sure I can access a mug shot." He opened Angie's computer and logged in to the state database. "Why?"

"Because if he was in my office, he was coming after me. Given what they knew about my life, he may have been following me for a while."

Jacob nodded slowly, clicking to the search page. He should have thought of that sooner. When Phelps's most recent mug shot loaded, he turned the screen toward Ivy.

She squeezed the water bottle, the plastic crinkling in her grasp. "I'm about 90 percent certain he's the cop that pulled me over." She leaned closer to the screen. "Take away the beard, trim the hair a bit… That's a pronounced widow's peak, almost exactly like the guy who came after me." With a shudder, she turned away and walked back to the window.

There was no doubt this entire operation was coordinated, and it had the fingerprints of Sienna Davies all over it. If this went well, they might wind up taking down a senate candidate and a contract killer with one blow of the ax.

Jacob took another photo, then glanced up at Ivy, who was pulling back the curtain to peek outside. If only he could guarantee this information would make her safe. If only—

"Jacob!" Her voice was so high-pitched he nearly dropped his phone as she whirled and raced for the door. "The horse barn is on fire!"

The horses! Ivy was out the door and down the porch steps in a full sprint. Shiloh was in the barn. If Jacob lost that horse, it would destroy him.

Thick smoke rolled out of the huge open doors on the front of the barn and raced away on the wind, chasing the storm. The horses whinnied and neighed their agitation and fear, but so far, none seemed to be in physical distress. There was time. She had to get in there and open those stalls. To save the animals. To spare Jacob more pain.

Her hand was on the corral gate when a strong arm encircled her waist and hauled her backward, nearly dragging her off her feet.

Too late, she realized this could have been a trap. Twisting and flailing, she tried to elbow her attacker. Where was Jacob? Why wasn't he intervening?

"Ivy!" Jacob's voice broke through, louder than the horses, close to her ear. "Stop. It's me."

The relief was short-lived. She was safe. His horses weren't. As his grip eased, she lunged for the corral gate again. "We have to—"

"No. *I* have to. *I'm* going in." He nudged her aside and unlatched the gate. "The way this fire is burning, somebody set it. From here it looks like hay bales dragged into the center aisle. Get in the house. Lock the doors. This could be an attempt to draw you out." Without waiting to see if she obeyed, he shut the gate and ran across the corral toward the barn.

New flames licked out of the haymow over the barn door. If someone had deliberately started a fire on both levels, there was no way he'd be able to get the horses out in time. He'd have to calm them and get them headed in the right direction. The roof could fall in. The horses could trample him.

Ivy slipped through the gate and shut it behind her, then ran for the barn door just as Jacob disappeared into the thick smoke. She would not let him handle this alone.

Pounding feet raced toward her as she neared the door, and a huge shadow broke through the smoke. Jumping to the side, she narrowly missed getting mowed over by the massive roan that had drawn Wren's attention earlier.

Wren. She said a quick prayer of thanks that her daughter was safely away from the house and barn with Angie and Linc.

Listening to make sure no more horses were charging out, she edged to the side of the door, pulled in a deep breath of smoke-tinged air and dove into the barn. Smoke stung her eyes and she crouched, trying to get below the rolling billows. Her lungs screamed that she'd held in air too long for her pounding heart to handle, but she dove deeper, barely able to see in the darkness. The electricity must have been one of the first casualties of the fire.

Feeling her way, trying to hear the horses over the flames roaring in the haymow above, Ivy reached a stall where a frantic gray hoofed the floor and reared. Standing to the side, she threw open the stall and prayed the horse would bolt for the open barn door.

It did, shaking its head as it vanished where the smoke was a lighter color, tinged by the outside light that did little to combat the dark smoke.

One more stall on this side. The smoke was too thick for her to see Jacob, the sounds of the frantic horses and the roaring flames too deafening for her to hear if he was nearby.

Air first. She needed air.

She dropped to her hands and knees, hay and oats digging into her palms, and heaved in the cleaner air near the ground. Still, the smell of horse and hay and gasoline choked her, but better than nothing. When she was ready, she crouched again, feeling for the last stall on the right. Her eyes burned and watered, further obscuring her vision, but she found it and slid the latch.

The horse inside was nothing more than a shadow in the smoke. It rushed out, galloping for freedom.

Ivy followed. *Lord, let Jacob already be out of here. Please.*

If something happened to him in the smoke and the fire…

There wasn't time to dwell on what it would mean if she lost him. The barn grew hotter. The smoke was so thick, she could no longer see her own feet, couldn't see farther than her hand in front of her face. Even the lighter smoke near the barn door was gone.

Ivy rested her hand on the stalls and let her fingers skim the wood so she wouldn't get turned around in the chaos.

Everything was dark and growing darker. Her lungs

were screaming. Sweat ran down her face and gathered everywhere that skin touched skin. She should be near the door.

Faintly, through the pounding in her ears and the fire overhead, a soft sound reached her. Then another.

Was that…?

She whipped around, her hand falling from the stall door.

There it was again.

A horse. Why hadn't Jacob freed the last horse? He'd been ahead of her in the smoke. Had he ducked out for air?

She turned toward the direction of the main door then looked back toward the sound of the pawing, whinnying horse.

It had to be Shiloh. Jacob's horse. The last stall on the left had always been hers.

Slipping to her hands and knees, Ivy took in the last good air she could find and turned back into the thick smoke. If she kept her right hand on the stalls, when she got to the back, she could follow the wall, release Shiloh and go out the sliding doors without having to endure the walk up the center aisle of the long building.

Lord, make this work. Don't let me leave my daughter behind.

She shouldn't do this.

But she couldn't let a horse suffer in the flames.

And she had no idea where Jacob was.

Closing her eyes against the stinging smoke, Ivy felt her way to the back of the building. When she found the metal wall that separated the stalls from the storage and office areas at the rear of the barn, she changed course until she ran straight into Shiloh's stall. She felt for the latch and fumbled with it, her pulse pounding a drum-beat in her ears and throbbing dark spots flashing in her eyes. She was running out of time. She had to release this…latch…

It slid to the side and Shiloh lunged out, frantic, racing for the front of the building.

Ivy wanted to breathe a sigh of relief, but that would be dangerous.

Something above her head toward the middle of the barn creaked and groaned. The ceiling. She didn't have much time.

But where was Jacob?

He wouldn't have left Shiloh behind.

She'd get out the back, get fresh air, run to the front of the building and see if he was there.

If not?

If not, she'd come back in for him.

Still feeling her way, she found the door that led into the back of the barn.

A large crack nearly drowned out all other sounds. A shower of flame and cinders crashed down into the middle of the barn, temporarily roiling the smoke as it fell.

Ivy nearly choked. *Please, God. Please don't let Jacob have been under that.*

She took another step, rushing for the back, and her foot caught. Her body pitched forward. She sprawled hard on the concrete, her hands scraping as she fell on top of something.

Something wearing a sage-green sweater.

Jacob. Her sharp inhale brought stinging, burning smoke into her lungs. She crawled around and ran her hand up his arm to his shoulder and neck, then rested her other hand on his chest. It seemed to take forever before his pulse thudded against her fingertips. Strong. Steady. His chest rose beneath her palm. Breathing. Slowly, but breathing.

He was alive, but there was no telling for how long or what damage had been done to knock him out like this.

And she was the only one who could rescue him.

Another crack and hot air blew against her, bringing burning cinders with it. The entire ceiling would come down soon.

He was bigger than her, deadweight and heavy. It might take more than she had left in her to drag him out. Ivy leaned over and tried to look him in the face in the red-tinged darkness. "Jacob!" She smacked his cheeks and got no response.

Another crash. She had no choice.

Pressing her cheek to the floor, she sought good air and took a deep breath. On her feet, she bent at the waist, found Jacob's booted foot and pulled. Her muscles, her eyes, her skin, her lungs—everything burned. Everything strained. Her running shoes slid on the concrete, but she braced and pulled again. One inch. Two.

Come on, Jacob. Get up.

They were never going to make it.

She backed through the door to the storage and office space, and the air cooled slightly as the smoke rolled toward the larger front door. Its foothold was still strong, though, and in the smaller space, the air grew more stifling. With the old office door closed and no windows, the darkness was heavy and thicker than the smoke could ever hope to be.

She kept hauling Jacob with her, straining against his weight with every inch.

Please, Lord. Please. The prayer pounded through her, in rhythm with her straining heart.

Her back collided with the huge sliding doors. Finally. Even though they were usually padlocked from outside, she could still get them out the smaller door to the left.

Settling Jacob's feet to the ground, Ivy felt for the door, for freedom, and finally located it in the blackness. The handle turned freely and she shoved.

The door didn't move.

Gasping for fresh air, for something, she threw her weight against the door, her shoulder shoving against the sturdy metal. It wanted to give, but a pressure outside held it firmly shut, as though something heavy had been leveraged against the door.

Her thoughts went fuzzy. Her arms and legs dragged at her, as though magnets were pulling her lower with a force she couldn't fight.

She had to…fight. To get to safety. So close.

The door… Jacob… She had to… *Wren*…

Her knees gave out and the darkness was complete.

TEN

Jacob grunted as something heavy dropped across his chest, making it impossible to breathe.

It was hot. So hot. Everything burned. His face. His lungs. His eyes beneath his closed lids.

He ached to go back to sleep. To kick off this weighted blanket and find cool air… To drift back into peaceful, heavy sleep.

His head pounded in rhythm with his heart. His jaw ached. Even his teeth hurt. Maybe he was sick. Had the flu. Or he was still in the hospital.

He'd dreamed about Ivy. That she'd visited him. That she—

Ivy.

In a rush of smoky air, the truth jerked him awake. The barn. On fire. Shiloh in her stall. He'd been going back for her when something had cracked him hard in the chin, causing his head to jerk back. Then, darkness.

He was still in the barn.

Jacob struggled and pushed, his arms too weak, his muscles refusing to cooperate. *Come on.* Whatever had fallen on him was heavy. Deadweight. Almost like…

A body.

He stopped shoving. Let his hands rest. A shoulder. An arm. There shouldn't be anyone else in the barn, unless...
No.

Jacob lay still, fighting shock and pain and a sudden wash of fear. *No fear. No fear.* Fear destroyed. Robbed you of your senses and your strength.

He needed both now.

Wrestling the pain in his head that pulsed through his entire body, Jacob managed to get his elbows beneath him and roll to the side, gently easing Ivy off his chest. He got a good deep breath and immediately wished he hadn't. Smoke choked him.

Something crashed in the barn area, quaking the building. There wasn't much time before the entire barn would drop on their heads. Whatever had started the fire, it was upstairs in the loft, where they stored hay, which burned fast and hot.

Leaning over Ivy, he rolled her onto her back and checked her pulse, then watched her chest rise and fall. Either someone had sucker punched her as well, or she'd given in to the smoke and fumes. Either way, he had to get her out and into fresh air before they both died in here.

And he would not leave his daughter an orphan, especially not when he'd just learned she existed. The three of them had a life together of some sort to work out. No one got to rob them of that.

Leveraging against the wall, he stood and stumbled the remaining few feet to the back door. When he tried to shove it open, something resisted from the outside.

Someone intended to burn them alive. Somehow, Sienna Davies and her crew had found Ivy.

He pushed again and the door gave slightly, just a crack but enough to let him feel fresh air on his arm.

Turning, he shoved with his shoulder and gulped the thin stream of cool, clear air that leaked through the opening.

It wasn't much, but it was enough to clear his head.

His cell phone. Linc was only a couple of miles away with Wren and Angie. He had to have seen the smoke, but if not... Jacob pulled the device from his back pocket and pressed the side button to light the screen.

No comforting glow lit the darkness. The screen was shattered, and the guts of the phone had probably been damaged when he fell.

The little bit of strength he'd managed to draw threatened to slip away. He couldn't do this. There was no way out.

Another roar. A rush of hot air flooded the room as the ceiling near the door behind him fell in. It was getting harder to breathe as the fire consumed the oxygen.

Reaching down, he grabbed Ivy and dragged her toward the back wall, as far from the fire as he could.

Fire craved oxygen. If he'd managed to open that door earlier, the fire would have leaped at the oxygen, flash broiling both of them.

Thank You, Lord.

But they were still only minutes from a horrifying death. There had to be a way out.

Wait. There was one in the old office. He prayed silently for strength and free passage as he grabbed Ivy and dragged her over the concrete, wincing against his pain and hers. The office door opened easily.

Jacob legitimately wanted to sink in relief. Just a few more feet. After pulling Ivy into the room, he shut the door behind them.

The room was hot but mostly free from the smoke and fumes that permeated the rest of the building. At the end of the room, the window stood just a couple of feet above the floor, and it slid sideways instead of raising. Enough room for them both to get out. *Thank You, Jesus.*

Leaving Ivy near the door, he stumbled the few feet across the room and shoved the window to the side, gulping the cool, damp night air that poured in. It felt like he'd been standing there for hours refilling his lungs, but it was probably only a few seconds.

Just give me enough to get Ivy out of here.

He headed back and hefted her in a fireman's carry, lifting her onto his shoulders. His muscles strained and screamed. He wavered on his feet. Each labored step punctuated a word of prayer. *Help. Me. Save. Her.*

Because if he lost Ivy again, he knew deep inside that he'd never be the same.

Leaning out the waist-high window, he used nearly everything left in him to shove Ivy forward, letting her slide to the damp ground.

His entire body shuddered as his muscles gave out.

The next thing he knew, he was facedown in the wet grass beside Ivy, gulping air.

They were still too close to the building, but there was nothing more he could do. His body was finished.

At the sound of shouts and running footsteps, he didn't even lift his head. It was over.

Ivy sat on the bench seat in the back of an ambulance, shivering. She gripped a silver thermal blanket around her neck with one hand and pressed the oxygen mask to her face with the other, taking in all she could get. The concentrated air was cold enough to burn her angry lungs, but she'd never take deep breaths for granted again.

Each inhale made her feel stronger, but it was probably just the euphoria her brain felt from being refueled.

She sat back against the wall of the ambulance and closed her eyes, letting the shouts of firemen and the chaos of the battle wash over her. Somewhere out there, Jacob was still being worked on by emergency workers. He'd been awake when they led her to the ambulance after she refused a gurney, but he'd been weak.

The vehicle rocked slightly, and Ivy opened one eye, turning her head to the door.

Jacob ducked his head and entered the ambulance slowly, an emergency worker right behind him. He raised one eyebrow when she looked up, then sat on the gurney in the center of the ambulance, facing her as an EMT prepped an oxygen mask and slid it onto Jacob's face, then took his blood pressure. Like her, he held the mask close, drinking oxygen like a dying man drank water after crawling across a desert. His color was gradually returning, but it was evident from the way he moved that he'd reached his physical limit.

The EMT finished his assessment and sat back slightly, the rip of the blood-pressure cuff loud in the ambulance as he pulled it away. "Your pressure's a little high, but that's nothing unusual. I'd recommend both of you get checked out at the hospital. There's no telling what you inhaled in there, and I'm pretty sure neither of you wants to suffer any longer than you have to if we can do anything about it."

Ivy shook her head. She did not want to go to the hospital. Clearly, the people Ross Evans had hired to kill her had found her. She needed to grab her daughter and run.

But before she could speak, Jacob laid a hand on her knee and pulled his mask away from his face. "Agreed.

We're ready to roll when you are." When Ivy started to speak, his fingers tightened, a silent *no*.

What did he know that she didn't? She wanted out of this ambulance. Wanted to find Wren. Where was her daughter?

The EMT didn't seem to notice their unspoken conversation. He stowed his equipment and turned to Jacob. "I'll grab the rest of the gear, get my partner and we'll get moving."

As he climbed from the ambulance, Jacob said, "Can you shut the door behind you?"

The EMT hesitated, then shut the rear door after he exited.

The outside sounds of firefighters at work dimmed, overtaken by the hum of the ambulance engine and the lifesaving equipment surrounding them.

Ivy started to speak, but Jacob held up a finger, listening. When he seemed satisfied that no one was near, he leaned closer and pulled his mask away again, speaking before she could. "We have to get out of here. The easiest way is in this ambulance. It's like an escort to the hospital. You're safer there. Security guards. Easier to protect you."

"Wren…" The name was muffled in the mask as she choked on the smoke and fire in her throat, both from the flames and from her desperate need to know her daughter was safe.

"Linc is with Wren and Angie." His whisper was labored, as though each breath cost him. "He'll make sure they're safe. He's smart enough to see the fire and get them out of here."

It was cold comfort. Her baby might be safe, but she wasn't in her mama's arms.

And no one would protect her like her mama.

He grabbed her hand and squeezed. "Ivy, I need you to trust. Not just Linc, but God. Nobody's going to love Wren more than He does."

The mild rebuke might as well have been a slap. Ivy tried to pull her hand away, but he held on. And as he did, the truth took hold.

Jacob was right. The One who had eyes on Wren at all times was the One she could truly trust. *Please, God...* It was all she had.

But she knew He heard.

If only that fact brought her more peace than she felt now.

She nodded slowly. "You're right." But a sudden thought ripped away her peace. She dragged the mask from her face and let it hang at her neck. "Jacob. The files. We have to—"

The expression on his face stopped her cold. His jaw tightened and his eyes narrowed.

He didn't have to speak the words.

"Jacob. No." They were gone. While Jacob and Ivy had been fighting for their lives in an inferno, someone had bolted with the files they'd risked everything to retrieve.

"I'm sorry. I bucked the medics and told them I had to go inside before I let them bring me out here. They weren't happy about it." He glanced away, then looked back, dipping his head so she was forced to meet his gaze. "I took photos of most of the pages with my phone. It was busted during the fire, but I'm almost certain our tech guys can access the data on it." He seemed to gain steam as he spoke, his words coming faster, his breathing easier. He was in full investigative mode. "The instant I get to a landline, I'll call Linc and have him send someone we trust to come and get it. If we do that fast enough, we can beat the bad guys to those safe-deposit boxes. Remember, we'll be able to get warrants. They won't. And without some sort of official paperwork with which to gain access from the bank—"

"You're forgetting one of the guys might be a federal marshal. And Evans likely has connections who can get him a warrant."

His eyebrows drew into a dark V. "I haven't forgotten." With a long exhale, he glanced toward the door. "I saw Shiloh in the corral." He grabbed her other hand in his, drawing both of their clasped hands together between their knees. "Thank you."

Ivy swallowed hard. Shiloh meant the world to Jacob. Always had. He'd trained that horse with his grandfather the summer before Jamison Garcia had passed away. "When I realized she was still there and I could save her, there was no way I was leaving her behind."

He drew the inside of his lower lip between his teeth, lowering his gaze to stare at their hands. "You were headed out when you realized she was in there."

"I was."

"You know…" He winced, his forehead furrowing into deep lines. "If you hadn't gone back for Shiloh…"

Ivy's grip on his hand tightened. The hum of the ambulance, the dull din of the firefighters still battling the blaze outside as they worked against the wind… All of it faded.

If she hadn't gone back for Shiloh, then she never would have stumbled over Jacob. He'd be dead.

She cleared her throat and stared at the top of his head, not willing to pursue that line of thinking. Her heart was getting too used to him, was too drawn to his presence.

Remembering who he'd once been to her, how much they'd planned, wondering why she couldn't simply let go of her fear and love him the way she once had.

Why? Because today had proven that, at any moment, she could lose him. She'd already grieved him once, and he'd still been walking the planet somewhere. If something took her permanently away from him...

Her heart would never recover. "What happened to you in there?"

"Someone hit me. How they managed to get in such a square blow in that darkness, I'll never know." He worked his jaw back and forth, wincing slightly. "It'll hurt worse in the morning."

"They blocked the back door."

"Yes."

The goal had been to burn them alive. Ivy shuddered and pulled her hands from Jacob's, wrapping her arms around her stomach. "All to protect their name. And to get their hands on stolen money that Mr. Mendez probably doesn't even have anymore."

"People will do a lot for power."

She rocked back and forth, trying to shove the fiery, dark smoke from her mind. There had to be a way to banish it forever, to keep it from coming back later and haunting her nightmares.

The ambulance rocked slightly as the driver's door slammed.

"We must be getting ready to move out." Jacob reached over and buckled Ivy in, then slid gingerly around to sit beside her, securing his own belt.

She laid her head against his shoulder. It didn't matter that he could never be hers again. Although he didn't act like what had happened with Wren bothered him, there was no doubt he would be angry once they were out of danger and the threat on her life was over.

None of that mattered, though. Right now, she needed to know he was real and he was beside her. Tomorrow, she'd worry about the future.

He tilted his head so his temple rested against her hair. "It's going to be okay."

The sound of the engine changed, and the ambulance lurched forward, throwing Ivy hard against Jacob's shoulder. She sat up quickly and looked around. "Where's the other EMT?"

Her head whipped back and hit the side wall when the vehicle hit a bump in the driveway. She cried out with the shock of it.

Jacob leaned forward, eyes narrowed as he stared at the front of the vehicle. When he looked at her, the dark expression in his gaze told her what she didn't want to know.

Something was very wrong.

ELEVEN

Jacob flexed his fingers and forced himself to plan, not to react. Linc had warned him, and it was time to listen.

Jacob might not be an emergency worker, but he knew how protocol worked. Unless there were serious extenuating circumstances, no driver would leave without his partner. Not only would he not leave a man behind, but he also wouldn't take off with patients in the back unsecured and with no one to care for them.

He had no doubt there was only one person in the front. He'd only heard one of the doors slam.

Ivy bounced into him again as the ambulance hit another rut in the driveway. He put an arm around her to steady her, and she looked up into his eyes. "You don't have your gun, do you?"

He shook his head slowly. Since Wren was in the house, he'd secured it in the safe in the ranch office almost as soon as they'd walked through the front door. "I didn't expect to need it." But he should have. He never should have let home and the ranch lull him into a false sense of security.

The vehicle made a sharp turn and the ride smoothed out. They were on the private paved road that headed to the ranch now. He had to find a way to stop this vehicle quickly. He knew the land around the ranch better than he knew the floor plan of his own home. Once they were on the main road, their chances of escaping in the darkness without getting killed by the bad guy or injured in the treacherous land near the canyon dropped with every passing mile.

But how could he stop this vehicle?

There was a small pass-through that led to the main cabin, but its positioning behind a counter with a cabinet over it would make it hard for him to do enough damage with his fist or arm to force the driver off the road.

Eventually, someone would figure out the ambulance was missing and they were, too. Emergency vehicles were tracked by GPS, so the minute they deviated from a planned route, alarm bells would go off somewhere, likely at central dispatch. And with a radio in the vehicle, their "chauffeur" could monitor most emergency traffic.

That meant that, wherever they were headed, they weren't going to be in this vehicle for long.

He still saw nothing that he could use as a weapon. He needed to pull some reconnaissance as well, see what they were up against. And as much as he wanted to protect Ivy, it would take both of them to get out of this alive.

Unbuckling his restraint, Jacob eased to the edge of the bench seat and turned toward Ivy. He kept his voice low, trying to keep the driver from hearing. "I need you to go through all of the drawers and cabinets you can access. If you have to break into something, we'll deal with the fallout later. I need a way to stop the driver."

Her mouth opened as though she was going to argue, but then she seemed to think better of it and freed herself from her seat belt. She slid over to the gurney to search the other side of the ambulance as they rounded a corner. Ivy swayed, bracing herself on Jacob's shoulder and on the small counter.

He reached up and laid his hand on hers for only a moment. "Be careful." He slid down the gurney to look out the back. Sure enough, there was a car behind them, keeping pace. He couldn't prove it, but he was almost certain whoever was driving that car was in on their kidnapping.

It had been a vain hope that their driver was acting alone.

And if the driver was smart, he knew Jacob wouldn't go passively. Might as well make himself known.

In the small space, he squeezed past Ivy and peered into the window that looked into the cab.

The driver was a man who was definitely not an emergency worker. He had on a black hoodie, and he pushed the ambulance at speeds that couldn't possibly be safe. He caught Jacob's eye in the rearview and smirked, then turned his attention back to the road, navigating a curve fast enough to throw Jacob to the side.

Jacob knew that curve. They had about one minute before they hit the main road.

The man laughed loud enough to be clearly heard through the closed window.

Jacob caught himself on the wall and refused to make a sound. No way would he give that man the satisfaction of speaking, of begging for their lives, or trying to bribe him into freeing them.

"Got it." Ivy's voice was low, and it held a thread of satisfaction.

Jacob dropped below window level and turned toward Ivy, who was hefting a large orange backpack onto the gurney. Somehow, she looked triumphant and vulnerable at the same time, as though she was strong enough to rescue herself but their teamwork would make it all easier.

If it took everything he had left in him, he would win this war for her.

With an arched eyebrow, Ivy pulled five emergency road flares from the bag and laid them on the gurney between them.

Jackpot.

Of course, an ambulance would have a roadside emergency kit. Jacob actually smiled. They were going to get out of this, one battle at a time. First, they'd stop this ambulance. Then, they'd deal with the vehicle trailing them.

Drawing the flares to him, he weighed them in his palm, trying to gauge the best way to use them. The small window that led to the ambulance's cab and the cabinets in front of it wouldn't allow him to directly reach the driver, but if he lit those flares and tossed them in, it should be enough to distract him. Best-case scenario, the smoke would force him off the road.

Jacob and Ivy simply had to survive the ensuing accident and get a head start on their pursuers.

So many variables. But there was no more time to plan. If he hesitated and they reached their destination, then the number of unknowns grew.

Their fight for freedom had to start now.

"What are we doing?" Ivy eased closer, her face set in that determined mask he'd seen earlier, the one that said she'd shoved her emotions into the pit of her stomach and was ready for action. Her game-day face.

Her home-run face.

How he loved that face.

More than that face. Everything about her.

He loved Ivy. He had never stopped loving Ivy.

There could not have been a worse time to figure that out. Right now, he needed his head engaged, not his heart. If he let his heart run the show, he'd get them both killed. Because his heart wanted to wrap his arms around her and pretend he could shield her from whatever came through the back of that ambulance next.

His head knew that would be deadly. He needed to treat Ivy like a teammate in this plan, not let his emotions go wild with fear over losing the woman he loved.

"Jacob?"

The ambulance hit a pothole, throwing Ivy toward him. Instinctively, he dropped the flares and braced his arm around her, drawing her closer.

This was the exact reason he had to get moving. He rested his forehead against hers for a moment then pulled away, grabbing the flares from where they'd bounced around on the gurney. "Get back onto the bench seat and buckle in. Strap in as tight as you can, then start lighting flares and passing them to me."

This was their one shot.

He eyed the bag she'd discarded by the gurney. He had no idea what was in it, but if they had to hike out the way he suspected they would, it could prove useful. "Bring the bag."

Ivy nodded, then resumed sitting and locked her seat belt into place. She threaded her left arm through one of the backpack straps and then picked up one of the flares and prepared to light it. Her lips moved slightly. She was praying.

He should be, too. But the only words he could muster through his frantic, adrenaline-fueled thoughts were *God, help us.*

He pulled in slow, deep breath after slow, deep breath until he was ready to go on the offensive. When his hands were steady and his mind clear, he maneuvered in the tight space until he was at the side of the window, just out of the driver's view if he glanced in the mirror.

When he looked back at Ivy, she was watching, waiting for his signal.

Jacob nodded.

He braced himself as he took the flare she'd lit and shoved it through the opening.

The driver screamed a string of unintelligible words that Ivy probably didn't want to decipher. As quickly as she could, she lit more flares and passed them to Jacob.

Through the window, smoke filled the cab of the ambulance.

The vehicle swerved in a sickening S. Left, then right.

Tires squealed and the engine revved.

Ivy kept her eyes shut, her stomach rocking with the careening vehicle. *Jesus. Jesus. Jesus.* There was nothing but His name. He knew what her heart was screaming.

Another jerk right. A horrifying splintering sound. The vehicle tilted forward and stuttered rapidly, as though it kept striking something as it plunged. The gurney banged into her knees. Her leg jerked in reflex.

The ambulance jolted hard to a stop, throwing Ivy forward. The seat belt dug into her shoulder as her upper body whiplashed.

Her eyes flew open as the lights flickered, then went dark. The silence was as complete as the darkness. No engine. No humming equipment. No nothing.

Only silence.

Jacob!

Ivy fumbled for her seat belt and scrambled up, falling over the gurney. They had come to rest at a forward tilt and listing to the left. "Jacob!" Her voice shredded on the ragged shriek, her throat like broken glass.

"Shh." Immediately, a hand was on her shoulder. Jacob urged her up, toward the rear of the ambulance. "We have to get out of here. Now. Quietly. There was a vehicle tailing us, and I don't know how many people were in it or how long it will take them to get down here."

His voice was strained, raspy from the fire. They were both still weak from their earlier ordeal in the barn. Now they were in the thick of another life-and-death struggle.

Everything hurt, but she shoved aside the pain. For Wren. She had to keep pushing forward. Her daughter needed her. Ivy slid the heavy backpack onto both shoulders and let Jacob push her toward the dim light that filtered in the door windows. She found the latch in the darkness and forced open the door.

"There might be a drop. Be careful getting out. Hit the ground running to your left and I'll catch up to you. Don't stop unless you hear me tell you to. Take cover anywhere you can."

She didn't want to leave him behind, but she had no choice. Hesitating could get them both killed. She climbed out the door then dropped out, hitting hard on the ground several feet below. The impact jolted her body, but she forced herself to run, stumbling over rocks and crashing into small trees as she flew downhill through the underbrush.

Her eyes began to adjust to the darkness after a moment, and she could make out the individual shapes of the landscape in the starlight of a moonless night.

The ambulance had come to a stop in the deep ra-

vine that ran along the private road leading to the ranch.
They'd explored the ravine many times. It wound its way
along the canyon, parallel to the rim, before sinking into
the canyon itself. She'd hiked it with Jacob's family more
than once, but it had been years, and in the dark, finding
a trail was next to impossible.

Ivy stopped running and braced against a large rock,
her heart pounding so loudly she could hear it. The ranch
was two to three miles behind her. Jacob's directions had
her running down into the canyon instead of back toward
the ranch and safety.

So that's what he was thinking…

From somewhere above, a car door slammed. Another
followed, and voices drifted through the sparse trees, the
words indistinguishable.

No. No. No. Jacob had said someone was following
them, but she'd hoped he was wrong.

Maybe it was rescue. Maybe the car behind them had
seen the ambulance careening and was here to help.

But they'd been on the private ranch road. Random
passersby were rare.

They couldn't take the chance.

Something heavy moved nearby, breathing deeply. She
hiked the backpack higher on her shoulders and tightened
the straps, prepared to run.

"Ivy." Jacob's voice floated to her.

"Here. To your right." She swallowed her fear and
bucked up. This wasn't the time for panic. "We're bound
to be close to the trail." He was going to take them down
into the canyon, away from the ranch, guessing that their
pursuers would assume they'd run for familiar safety.

He reached her and rounded the rock, dropping to the
ground beside her.

In the cool darkness, as her eyes grew even more accustomed to the dim light, she could just make out his face. The lines in his forehead were deep, but they weren't from worry. They were from pain. She'd seen that look before, when he'd been carted off the football field with a dislocated shoulder. "What's wrong?"

"We have to keep moving. Quietly. Don't let them hear you." His left hand found hers, and he squeezed her fingers. "They'll check the vehicle first. It will take them a minute to get down to it, but that's not much time." He breathed in sharply, then exhaled slowly. "Hopefully they'll think we doubled back to the ranch or we're climbing toward the road."

"You are not okay."

The two voices shouted at each other. They'd reached the ambulance.

"We have to move." Jacob pushed off the rock and tugged at her hand.

Ivy looked back as two flashlight beams crisscrossed through the thin trees, bouncing as their pursuers tried to determine which direction they'd fled.

She stumbled over something in the path and Jacob's grip on her hand tightened, then he stepped in front of her. "Pay attention." The command was sharp.

But he was right.

They pushed forward, Ivy watching her feet as she trailed closely behind Jacob. This was his land, and he knew the way better than she ever would.

The voices faded. The flashlights grew dimmer. It felt like hours, but it was probably more like minutes before Jacob stopped abruptly and backed up a step, colliding with her.

Her head jerked up, a "what?" on her lips, but it died

before it could greet the air. In front of them, a huge pile of rocks blocked their way.

She sucked in a couple of deep breaths as Jacob took one more step back, then looked right and left. It seemed the right face of the ravine had fallen in, but there was a narrow passage against the wall.

"Did we miss a turn?" It had been years since she'd been out in the canyon, but she'd have remembered this blockage in the trail.

"No. It would be impossible to get turned around in the ravine. It's worse. All that rain earlier was a lot at once. Rock slides. We'll have to keep close to the left face of the ravine as we move down. And pray the whole wall doesn't rain down on our heads."

TWELVE

Jacob had done a lot of "dumbest things ever" in the last couple of days, but this one? This one might be the one that got him and Ivy killed. They were heading below the rim of the Grand Canyon—even for one night—with no supplies, no resources. Both of them were still exhausted from their ordeal at the barn, oxygen-starved, in pain... and he was fairly certain his arm was fractured from the wild ending to their ambulance ride.

They were at the far edge of his family's ranch land. The trailhead he was searching for was off the map and hard enough to find in the daytime. On a moonless night, it was going to take a lot of help from a God who was able to see a whole lot more than they could.

A shout echoed in the distance behind them.

He stopped and turned back. They had made it far enough to be out of range of those flashlight beams, but the way they cut through the darkness in the distance was still too close for comfort.

Ivy stopped beside him. The only sound in the near darkness was her breathing, rapid but steady. They both needed water and rest and probably more oxygen. They definitely needed warmer clothing. As adrenaline wore off, the chilled air on the back side of the front that had swept through grew more pronounced. While it hadn't dropped to freezing, hypothermia was still a very real threat, and they were both dressed for indoors. Neither had grabbed a jacket on their run toward the burning barn, but thankfully he'd pulled on boots.

Worse, they had none of the basics for survival. Water? Food? A way to communicate?

Nothing.

The flashlights bobbed and bounced, then separated. One climbed toward the road and the other angled away from them.

At least one thing was going the way he'd planned. Heading down the ravine toward the canyon would likely prove to be dangerous in the long run, but it had saved their lives in the short term.

They may not have all the time in the world, but they had just bought themselves valuable minutes. Cradling his arm against his stomach, he tapped Ivy with his good hand. "Let's go."

"You're sure about this?" The ordeal was wearing on her, or she wouldn't have asked. She'd never been one to reveal weakness easily.

"Honestly? No. But it's the best I've got right now." They'd hiked deeper into the ravine, which was shallow on the canyon side. The walls to their left and toward civilization grew higher with every step of their descent. In essence, until they found the trail that branched down into the canyon, they were bottled in.

They couldn't debate a course of action for long. If their pursuers figured out they'd headed for the canyon, they'd have nowhere to hide. "We have to keep moving." He tugged at her wrist to urge her to start walking.

They could talk in low whispers, but they had to move while they did.

She stumbled, then started walking in front of him, slowly, feeling her way as she went. "Jacob." His name was a harsh hiss. Hard to tell if it was fear or frustration. "I don't know how to find the trail."

"About a mile in, there are two boulders that mark the head of the trail."

She walked several steps before she spoke again. "Think we can wait them out without hiking directly into the canyon?"

"No."

"Then canyon it is." She seemed to find some sense of bravado again. Her pace picked up slightly, though she continued to ease her way forward.

He'd prefer to lead the way, but it seemed she was only going to move ahead if she had some sense of control.

Jacob could appreciate that. He breathed in and out through clenched teeth, every step jarring the arm he tried to hold immobile against his stomach. Ivy had grabbed the kit from the ambulance, but there was no time to stop now and dig through it for wraps or pain pills.

Besides, his mouth was too dry to swallow them, anyway.

Ivy glanced over her shoulder. "You're going to tell me you know of a cabin down here, I hope. One where someone just happened to leave out an entire buffet and plenty of ice-cold water."

He almost smiled. Stress and sarcasm were sisters in Ivy. "Not quite. But barring another rock slide in our way, there's that cave."

"I forgot about the cave."

Jacob's foot landed on a rock and tipped him sideways, jarring blue-white pain into his hip and his arm.

It mimicked the pain that memories rocked through his heart. It had been a hike on this trail to that cave that had made him realize he was in love with Ivy Bridges and wanted to spend the rest of his life with her. She'd come home with him over fall break just a couple of months after they met and had taken a day hike with his family. They'd reached the cave around lunchtime and had ducked inside, out of the sun, for sandwiches and water before the hike back up.

Ivy had been standing near the cave's narrow entrance, laughing at something Angie said. The way the sunlight angled in and hit her face…

That was the moment he'd lost his heart to her permanently. And whether he wanted to admit it or not, he'd never gotten it back from her.

He swallowed, even though his mouth was almost too dry to support the action. Pain and darkness and exhaustion did not make for good mental ramblings. He needed to focus on their current situation, not on their past or on a future that could never be, not as long as Ivy let fear rule her world.

And not as long as he had to sort out his feelings about what she'd done by keeping him from Wren.

"You know…" His voice was dry and cracking. "The longer we're out here, the better our eyes adjust."

"Is that your current silver lining?"

"At the moment, y—"

She stopped so suddenly he ran into her back and gasped at the jolt to his arm. Whatever she said, it was lost in the momentary flood of pain into his brain.

"What?"

Ivy pointed at something to their right. "Two boulders mark the head of the trail? I hope that's them."

He followed the line of her arm and exhaled in relief. It was them. Another mile, no more than an hour at their current slow pace, and they'd at least have shelter.

Ivy shivered and started walking again, a little bit faster this time. She had to be colder than he was.

"You okay?" What he really wanted to say was that he was sorry he'd gotten them into this mess. That he hadn't seen the barn fire coming. That it would be his fault if they didn't make it out of this to see their daughter again.

"Just hoping the trail isn't as steep in reality as it is in my memory. I mean, I can see fairly well by the stars now, but not well enough to navigate a sharp angle."

Jacob gritted his teeth. If she was deflecting the question, then she was more miserable than he'd initially thought. Ivy didn't handle weakness well. She hid behind bravado and feigned misunderstanding. Always had. Up until they'd parted, it had been the one thing he could never get her to understand and it drove a wedge between them. He'd wanted to know how she truly felt, wanted her to run to him when she needed someone. She preferred to bottle her emotions up and handle them on her own.

Maybe that was part of the reason she'd chosen not to tell him he was a father. She'd said it was to allow him to live the life he felt led to leave, the one he'd chosen. Making the decision for him was her way of handling it herself.

He shook his head, wincing as the motion jerked through his shoulder. Now wasn't the time for that. Now was for survival. "Not too steep. It gentles down and doubles back over itself a few times. The cave is after the second turn."

No need to remind her that the entrance was barely narrow enough to squeeze through. He prayed he could find it in the darkness when exhaustion and pain were rapidly robbing him of his strength.

They hiked for so long, he lost track of time and distance. Even the stars seemed to fall closer, as though the dome of the sky was growing as heavy as his body. If they didn't find shelter soon, he might not be able to walk much farther.

From somewhere in the distance behind him, a lone voice shouted.

Maybe he was hallucinating.

But Ivy stopped and turned. Even in the dim starlight, he could read the terror on her face.

Their attackers were headed their way.

Ivy didn't dare speak. That shout had been at a distance, but with the echoes and the way the ravine funneled sound, there was no way to tell what distance. No way to tell if their pursuers were in the ravine or had discovered the trail and headed down behind them.

Surely they hadn't.

She didn't have to ask Jacob if he'd heard it, too. In the dim light, the tight lines in his forehead told her everything he wasn't saying.

Ivy started walking again, picking her way down the trail. The way was narrow, against a sheer rock face on one side and only a few feet from a ledge on the other. Her night vision was getting better with every minute they walked in the darkness.

She adjusted the backpack into a more comfortable position. Surely that cave couldn't be much farther.

Then again, they could have passed it days ago.

Because it felt like she'd been walking, jaw clamped to keep her teeth from chattering, for her entire life. There was nothing before this. There might not be anything after it.

But there was Wren. Imagining Wren at the end of the trail, Ivy walked on. The only reason she was upright and moving was her daughter. Exhaustion and cold had numbed her body long ago.

She ought to be grateful. The numbness probably masked the pain. The only thing that hurt was her lungs. They burned with every breath, warning her that she wasn't getting nearly as much oxygen as she needed.

With another stunted breath, she continued the silent prayer she'd been pounding out with each footfall. So far, God had answered. She hadn't turned her ankle or pitched over the side of the canyon.

She tried to concentrate on the dark beauty around her to keep from focusing on death hounding their heels. Above her, the stars were so close she could almost pull them down and use them to light her way. They ran all the way to the place where canyon met sky, where the walls of one of the greatest sites in nature blotted them out.

So many people pictured the Grand Canyon as a narrow slash in the land, but it was so much more. It was a wide-open, intricately carved system of gorges and canyons and ravines, some stark and empty, some dotted with fir trees. While the darkness hid all of that, her mind's eye remembered.

"Ivy." Jacob's voice stopped her. He'd walked forward silently for so long she'd almost forgotten he was there. "I found it."

She'd been so busy studying the sky and watching her

feet, she'd neglected to search for shelter. Resting her hand on the rock face, she turned gently.

Jacob was several feet behind her, close to the canyon wall. He motioned her forward, his arm a shadow in the starlight. "If this isn't it, it's shelter, at least."

And then, he disappeared. It was almost as though he'd walked straight through the rock into another world. Narnia in Arizona.

Stepping closer, she found a narrow slit in the rock face, barely big enough for a body to squeeze through sideways. She angled and slipped in. "I hope there's not a bear in here."

"You're more likely to find a rock squirrel." Jacob's voice echoed in the pitch-dark interior of the cave.

The darkness had weight. The air was heavy and still. It felt like a thousand eyes watched from the inky blackness, ready to pounce.

A slight whimper leaked out as Ivy exhaled, fear suddenly real enough to make her turn her feet toward the door so she could bolt into the night. At least out there, the stars offered light.

"Ivy." Jacob was close. His hand found her wrist, and he pulled her close, wrapping one arm around her and holding her to his side. "You're okay. We're safe for now."

She wanted to bury her head in his shoulder, close her eyes and pretend it was true. But when she tried to move, he held her firm.

A shiver ran through her, but she wasn't sure if it was from the cold or from the man. "What's wrong?" So many times in the past, she'd just known when something was bothering him. And right now? She felt it with certainty.

He withdrew his arm but stayed close, saying nothing.

The fear rushed back, but she clamped her teeth together and prayed. Terror couldn't take her out now. There were a lot of physical attacks to battle. And Jacob—

Wait. Jacob hadn't reached out to her with both arms or both hands since they started their trek. *That* was the thing that nagged at her. "You're hurt."

In the stillness, his breathing was louder, and she could just pick up the ragged catch at the end of each inhale. She'd heard that same catch when he'd dislocated his shoulder in college.

"How bad is it?" He had internal injuries from his time overseas, that much she knew. Was he bleeding inside? Was this something he should have told her sooner? "Jacob. How bad?" She tried to keep the frantic edge out of her voice, but it knifed its way out.

"Just my arm. I think it's fractured. Nothing more."

Not life-threatening, but painful and possibly a big problem if they didn't get help soon. There was no telling what the pain was like—they were both physically drained and trekking in the cold through the Grand Canyon at night. This night was the definition of "harsh conditions."

But she might be able to help. "I grabbed that kit from the back of the ambulance, the one the flares were in. It's probably a roadside emergency bag, but if that's the case, then there might at least be solar blankets." Her car's kit had one, so it was possible. If only she'd grabbed the blanket from the ambulance.

Probably better that she hadn't. Bright silver moving in the starlight would have given them away immediately. "Let's see what's inside." It might be next to impossible in the dark, but it would give her something to do. Maybe it would take her mind off her body's screaming need for water. It had only gotten worse since they stopped walking.

He murmured something under his breath that was probably a prayer of thanks similar to her own. "At the least, there should be a flashlight and a first-aid kit."

"It would be a start."

"We'll sit and search." Jacob squeezed her shoulder once, then slid to the floor of the cave.

Sliding the bag from her shoulder, Ivy settled beside him and started patting pockets and netting, searching for a flashlight. They'd have to be careful. The light would glow in the cave's darkness and possibly leak out toward the entrance. If their pursuers were on their trail, a lighthouse wouldn't be a brighter beacon.

When her hands closed around a familiar metal cylinder, she closed her eyes in relief, though she didn't turn it on yet. Instead, she opened the bag and shoved the light inside, concealing the beam within the heavy canvas.

Even blocked, the light was a relief. Tangible hope.

She shifted the contents around. A couple more flares. Waterproof matches. And… "Jacob." His name was a whisper. She had to be hallucinating. There were pouches of water and an empty metal canteen, protein bars sealed in plastic bags with the air vacuumed out…and a first-aid kit. "It's not a roadside kit. It's a survival kit. But why would it be in an ambulance?"

She was literally aching for water, but she opted for practicality first. After opening the first-aid kit, she tore off strips of gauze and looped them over the flashlight until the beam was muted to almost nothing, though it was still enough to allow her to work.

"This is rough country. The snow can get heavy. It's probably a *just in case we ever get stuck in the middle of nowhere and have to wait for rescue* thing. But right now? It's a very good thing. A God thing." He took the pouch of water Ivy held out and tore it open, drinking deeply before he handed it back to her. "Your turn."

Ivy tried not to guzzle it all. Although it had a slightly stale taste from the pouch, it was a sweet balm to her dry, still smoky throat. Nothing had ever tasted better.

When she tried to hand it back to Jacob, he took it and held it. "Find some ibuprofen." While she dug in the first-aid kit to hunt for medicine and a fabric bandage, he resettled his position, probably trying to get more comfortable against the rock. "You know, there's a cave near the Awatubi-Sixtymile saddle that has a survival cache hidden in it. I was wishing the whole walk down here we were closer to it, but it's a three-day hike in and several days' hike from here."

"What's it for?" Jacob had always tended to talk more when he was uncomfortable. If he needed to tell a story to take his mind off his pain, she'd encourage it.

"A few years ago, a hiker went missing. Her brother and a park ranger went looking for her, and in the process, they busted up an operation illegally excavating antiquities and smuggling them out of the park. It was before I got here. Apparently, they took up shelter in a cave on the descent to Lava Creek during a storm while they were searching for the sister. Since the two of them got married, they hike down to Lava Creek on each anniversary and drop off emergency kits in a couple of the caves along the trail."

"That's cool." Ivy shoved aside the gauze that kept falling in her way. It was tough digging through the deep bag while holding the flashlight inside, but—

Jackpot. Two rolls of fabric bandages were nestled in

the bottom of the pack in a plastic bag. "I can make you a sling. As soon as I do that, I'll sort out the rest of what's in the bag, see if there are pain meds."

She set aside the bag, leaving the flashlight mostly concealed, and turned toward Jacob. "Let's see if we can at least make you more comfortable." If there was truly a fracture, then he needed more help than she could offer. But if she could alleviate some of his pain, she'd do whatever she could.

Ivy managed to fashion a makeshift sling, immobilizing his arm against his stomach.

After she'd tucked the last of the bandage securely into place, she located and passed on some ibuprofen, then sat back on her heels. "I didn't feel a break, but I'm no professional. I think you're right about fractured, maybe sprained."

"So how did you learn how to immobilize an arm?" Now that his arm was stabilized, some of the spark returned to Jacob's personality.

"I took some advanced first-aid courses before Wren was born." She wasn't going to take any chances that something could happen to her daughter. It might have been overkill, but feeling capable in the midst of her helplessness had given her peace. "It was—"

Jacob grabbed her wrist suddenly, shooting her a hard look. "Light."

There was no mistaking his meaning. Reaching into the bag, she punched the button on the flashlight, feeding the darkness. Her heart pounded.

From outside the cave, something shuffled. Gravel shifted.

Then silence.

THIRTEEN

The darkness in the cave was complete. The muted flashlight had reset Jacob's night vision, rendering him unable to see.

The sound came again. Something big was drawing near. If their pursuers spotted the entrance and shined their lights inside, there would be nowhere to run.

Rescue was up to him.

Him. The man with no weapon and an injured arm, who was already flagging from the smoke and heat of a barn fire.

The scraping inched closer.

Ivy's hand found his and held on. Both of them knew it. There was no fight.

Jacob prayed harder than he had all night, with his back literally to a wall.

Silence fell. It was somehow worse than the sound. Had they been found? Was danger about to pounce?

A softer sound drifted to them. Something was breathing. Huffing. And it wasn't human.

Thank You, Lord. They were safe. Sienna Davies was not about to charge in and wipe them off the planet.

His relief was short-lived. He could reason with a person, maybe. Could find a way to stall.

But elk, mountain lions or bears? While they tended to hesitate around humans, they acted on instinct and often attacked when threatened or hungry.

The only thing he could defend them with was a flashlight.

The creature sniffed at the entrance, likely picking up their scent. Thankfully, Ivy hadn't opened the sealed food yet.

But sometimes they associated humans with food...

The sniffing grew louder. The animal butted against the cave entrance.

Ivy inhaled sharply. "How do we fight this?"

His only defense was a very loud offense, although screaming would lead Davies straight to their hiding place. It would have to be a last resort if the animal came at them. Jacob stood and faced the threat. If it wanted Ivy, it would have to go through him. "If it gets in, skirt past me and get out."

"I'm not leaving—"

"You are." He'd rather die protecting her than live knowing he'd failed her. "Wren needs you."

That ought to silence her arguments.

She huffed nearly as loudly as the animal, but said no more. Instead, she stood behind him, one hand warm on his back.

For torturous moments, the creature pawed and huffed. As Jacob's eyes adjusted, he could see the shadow blocking the lower half of the light that leaked through the opening.

Every breath might be his last.

Finally, with a snort of frustration, the animal gave up,

too large to wedge into the opening. It lumbered away, heading back up the trail toward the trees.

Ivy melted against his back with an audible sigh, resting her head on his shoulder. "What was that?"

Jacob dropped his chin to his chest and gave himself a moment before he answered. "No idea." *However...* He almost smiled. Blessings didn't always look like blessings. "Whatever it was, it just saved our lives."

"I had a heart attack, Jacob." Ivy's whisper carried the full weight of her terrified sarcasm. "Tell me how that was a good thing."

As his adrenaline ebbed, a chill settled over him. He shivered, a cold, sharp feeling in his joints and his abdomen, where old injuries protested. Not wanting her to see how he was affected, he resumed sitting against the cave wall. "He headed toward the rim. Even if our friends managed to find the trail…"

Ivy actually chuckled as she sat beside him. "They won't tangle with a bear. They'll assume we wouldn't, either." She clicked on the flashlight, casting dim shadows through the cave.

It was impossible to get comfortable. Reaching behind him, Jacob pulled his busted phone from his back pocket. Maybe…

Holding his breath, he tapped the screen while Ivy leaned closer to watch.

Nope. Still a brick. He passed it to her. "Put it in the backpack. It's the only evidence we have left." If the memory was even accessible.

"Hopefully, we'll beat Evans to whatever is in those safe-deposit boxes." Ivy wrapped her arms around her knees. "I just want this to be over."

"We're safe for now." If they could avoid hypothermia. He didn't want to consider what the temperature might be.

"I should count my blessings?" Ivy smiled.

"Exactly." As he relaxed, his stomach reminded him that he hadn't eaten since a drive-thru lunch on the road from Landow. They both needed energy. "Want to hand over an energy bar?"

Ivy cut open the shrink-wrapped packet with scissors from the first-aid kit, then gave it to him. "Guess what I just found." With a flourish, she produced two palm-size packages and tossed one into his lap.

It was a thin plastic emergency blanket, like the ones the EMTs had given them earlier. Very few things would have made his shivering body happier. While it was no down-filled comforter, it helped hold in some of his body heat.

Ivy shivered, wrapped in her own blanket. They sat with their shoulders touching, silently eating. It wasn't much but, given the circumstances, it felt like a banquet.

When Ivy finished, she crinkled her wrapper and stowed it in the backpack, staring into the bag like it held all of the answers to this mess they were in.

Jacob polished off his energy bar and passed her the trash to put away. "You okay?"

"I'm...tired. And thinking. I know how they found me." She fiddled with the backpack strap. "I had a letter. In my purse. From you. The last one you ever wrote to me. I'm sorry."

"Sorry?" For what? For holding on to a piece of their past, of the love they'd shared? For running to him for help?

"Jacob, I know you were hurt overseas. Badly. And if something happens to you because of me..."

The words felt like stinging sleet against his skin. Somehow, Ivy knowing his greatest weakness hurt worse than his injuries. It tore the core of his being. He wasn't the strong man she once knew. And yet...

With her, he felt like that man. The more Ivy and Wren needed him, the more he'd leaned on God to protect all three of them. Maybe that was the point. It wasn't about Jacob and his strength. It was about God and His strength.

He needed to tell his story. While he'd talked about it in counseling, and briefly to Linc, he'd never laid it out to someone when the stakes were high. When they could reject him.

He needed Ivy to know the truth about how much his arrogance had cost him.

Maybe it was because, years ago, he'd have already told her everything, and he knew it deep inside.

So did she.

In the darkness between them, time no longer existed. It could have been today or years before, when she was the woman who loved him and knew him the best of anyone in the world. They were suspended in a moment that wouldn't let him keep his pain locked away from her any longer.

"It was a trip-wire IED in a village in Afghanistan."

It had been hot that day. Unbearably hot. They'd walked into the shade of trees in that village, grateful for some relief from the heat that had soared over one hundred degrees.

But their mission was serious. Intel said some insurgents had been slipping near the forward operating base, pulling recon. Possibly planning an assault.

So his team had headed out on patrol with infantry

from the base. Jacob had taken up the rear as they entered the village, watching for threats behind them. Specialist Brazier had shouted something he still couldn't remember, and the next thing Jacob knew, he was staring up at a crystal-blue sky through the overarching trees. His ears were ringing. His lower back and his abdomen felt like someone had lit a fire in his kidneys that might burn straight through him. Everything hurt.

Someone told him later that Brazier had spotted a trip wire and stopped, but Corporal Slade had been too close on his heels and knocked Brazier into the wire. They'd died instantly.

Through the dust that rained down and the whine in his ears, Specialist Dartwell was screaming. The infantry team that had already passed the IED raced back, radioing for help. Their medic stopped at Jacob, but his only visible injury was a cut on his hand, where he'd instinctively thrown up his arm to block the blast. Although his gut burned with white-hot pain, he went to help Dartwell, who'd taken shrapnel everywhere his body armor didn't cover.

Shrapnel that would have riddled Jacob had Dartwell not been between him and the blast. Blood poured from the younger man's neck, his carotid artery severed. So much blood. No way to stop it.

Jacob locked on the sight and couldn't look away. Couldn't move. The air around him was quicksand. Too heavy. Muffled. Weighing his thoughts.

The last thing he remembered was a medic grabbing him by the arm. The next was the white ceiling of a room at Landstuhl Regional Medical Center in Germany. The morphine in his system was ebbing, and everything from his rib cage to his toes screamed in pain. The concussive injuries from the force of the blast had moved like shock waves through him, breaking bones and rupturing internal organs. He'd nearly bled out into his own abdomen. Only the skill of the docs in Afghanistan had put most of him back together again.

Ivy's hand on his wrist, the very thing he'd craved lying in a hospital bed as he'd tried to remember who he was and what had happened, drew him into the present. He'd come to his senses with Ivy on his mind.

And now she was here and everything his morphine-dulled mind had cried for back then. In that haze, with his emotions unbound and his mental fences kicked down, all he'd wanted was her to walk up to the bed beside him, take his hand and give him something to live for.

Her acceptance and support lifted a guilt he'd carried since that day. Wiped away the deep, unspoken fear that she'd reject him for walking into the very situation she feared most, and for nearly dying.

For surviving while others didn't.

Once again, with his body aching and his defenses down, he knew where he wanted his relationship with Ivy to go. Since she'd reappeared the night before, every long-buried feeling he'd once felt had resurfaced. And knowing they shared a daughter...

Part of him wanted to be angry at her for withholding his child from him. But anger paled next to their fight for survival. He'd have to deal with the emotions eventually. There would be painful, honest conversations. But in the fight for her life, he was quickly learning that he needed her. That whether he was celebrating highs or fighting through lows, he wanted Ivy by his side.

The long-dead dreams they'd once held found new life in a bare, frigid cave.

Only one thing tempered his resurgent feelings.

Nothing he could do would change Ivy's fears. As long as they ruled her life, there was no future for them.

Only God could rescue her. Rescue their future. And until He did, Jacob could dream all he wanted, but Ivy would hold the keys.

Entwining his fingers with hers, Jacob closed his eyes and let his heart revel in this moment they did have. He knew Ivy wouldn't say anything. She'd let his story lie, would consider it and pray over it and over him. It was her way when he was hurting. To simply support him in whatever he needed. She'd listen when he was ready to speak again.

That would come later. They both needed rest if they were going to hike out of here in the morning.

But Jacob was going to pray until he fell asleep. He was going to keep praying from this moment forward.

Until God told him to stop, or until love cast out the last of Ivy's fears.

Ivy groaned and shifted, reluctant to open her eyes. She'd awakened a couple of minutes earlier, abruptly aware of her situation. There was no slow moment of realization. It smacked her in the face.

If she kept her eyes closed, she could pretend she was safe for one more minute, but the floor was too hard and her body ached too much to let her dive into make-believe.

So did her heart.

Jacob's pain had kept her awake for most of the night. Emotional and physical torment had poured from him as he'd told his story, seeming to heal something in him as he released the past. He'd fallen asleep shortly after, leaving her to process the divergent paths their lives had taken before coming together again.

Sometime in the middle of the dark, terrifying night, the truth had hit her. While she was caring for their very young daughter, Jacob could have died in an Afghan village or on the operating table in an army hospital. He could have been irrevocably torn from this world, just like her father had been.

It was the singular thing she'd feared most. The biggest reason she'd not followed him into his military journey. And her fear had cost both of them. The day they said goodbye, she'd lost him. He might not have died, but their relationship and their dreams had been slaughtered. Not by enemy fire, but by her fear.

She'd created the thing she'd been most afraid of. In doing so, she'd abandoned Jacob to suffer through a nightmare alone when she could have been by his side.

The truth gutted her. It had gnawed her heart the entire night, blending with their current danger to form a bitter pain.

And it had been a long night. Too many times, she'd peeked to find it was still dark. Morning had refused to come.

Edging one eye open, she prayed for daylight at the cave entrance.

This time, a hazy glow softened the mouth of the cave. She'd survived until morning. There was still time to make things right with Jacob. Maybe he'd never be able to trust her again, but she needed him to know she was immensely sorry for the pain she'd put him through and for the destruction she'd wreaked in their lives.

As soon as they were safely above the rim again, she'd tell him everything.

For now, they had to be more concerned with survival. Without pulling away from the rock, she turned her head to check on him.

He was gone. Only his plastic blanket lay beside her, a testament that she hadn't dreamed everything.

She sat up so quickly that the world rocked and tilted. The little bit of rest she'd gotten hadn't been enough to repair the damage done to her body the day before. Bracing her hands on either side of her hips on the cold stone floor, she tried to reset her bearings.

"I'm here." Jacob's voice came from the right.

He was sitting on the ground with the backpack resting between his knees. His grin was sheepish. "I was looking for more ibuprofen. Pretty sure mine wore off a couple hours ago."

She had no idea what time it was or when she'd handed him those first ibuprofen, but it had to have been long enough for the medication to quit his system. "In the first-aid kit, on the right side." Easing herself up to stand, she evaluated the muscles in her body.

Yep. They all hurt. Her throat was still raw, and her lungs still protested every breath. This was not the ideal physical condition to be taking on the Grand Canyon, but it wasn't like she could opt out of the hike. "How long do you think we walked last night?" The real question was "how long will it take to hike back out?"

Jacob tore open a small packet that held two pills, popped them in his mouth and chased them with water from their emergency stash. "I have no idea. Could have been hours. But I know this cave is only about two miles from the trailhead and then it's another mile or so to the main road." He passed her a pouch of water and an energy bar. "It's uphill all the way, though it's not a steep incline. And I don't have to tell you how I feel about running around in broad daylight when I don't know where my enemy is."

"Running around in the dark might be worse." Last night's flight had been so fast, she hadn't had time to consider the snakes and bugs and other critters that she might encounter on the trail. But after their close call with whatever hulking monster had wanted entrance to their hiding place the night before, those critters were at the forefront of her mind now.

"I hate having no good options." Using his uninjured arm, Jacob braced on the cave wall and eased up. His voice was bitter, as though he was finally feeling the full effects of their situation.

He was a take-control kind of guy. One who was used to being in charge. Being strategically blind to the outside world as well as injured and exhausted had to be taking a toll. Their uphill trek back to civilization would be slow going for both of them.

"Surely somebody has noticed we're missing, found the ambulance and figured out what happened. There will be a search, right?" In the bleak night, Ivy hadn't even considered that they weren't truly lost. There was a wrecked ambulance to point searchers in their general direction. "We could stay here and wait."

"We could. But we risk running out of what little bit of water we have in the meantime. If we head up, it might take us a while, but we'll eventually make our way out."

Chewing the energy bar, Ivy tried not to acknowledge that the water she'd had the night before and the pouch she held now weren't enough. She dragged the backpack closer and dug inside it. Six more four-ounce pouches of water and the same number of energy bars. Given their already weakened condition and the strenuous nature of the hike they were about to endure, they'd collapse from dehydration long before they starved. It happened fast in the canyon.

"There's another thing to consider." Jacob didn't look at her. He paced toward the mouth of the cave instead, almost as though he hated to give her more bad news. "If we encounter someone on the trail, we have no way of knowing if they're friendly or not."

Ivy sipped her water, taking it slowly. Maybe her body would believe there was more coming in than there actually was.

Yeah, it didn't work that way. "I need some good news, Mr. Sunshine."

"How about some motivation instead?" He walked back and crouched beside her. "As soon as we get back to civilization, I'll make you and Wren the breakfast I never got the chance to deliver on."

She'd been trying not to think about Wren. Not knowing where their daughter was, or if she was safe, had been further fuel to her raging midnight torment. It had been all too easy to think the worst.

Jacob held out a hand, palm up, took the wrapper she handed him and shoved it into the backpack. "Linc and Angie won't let anything happen to her."

She had to believe that. It was one more area where she didn't have a choice.

They finished their water in silence. It hardly slaked her thirst, but it would have to do. Both of them were reluctant to burn through their meager stash when they had no idea how long it would take them to make the trek to the rim.

"Well, let's head out." Jacob stood and reached for the backpack, but Ivy slid it out of reach with her foot.

"I'll carry it. You worry about nursing your arm."

A flicker of rebellion darkened his features, but Ivy didn't flinch. There was no way she would let him try to balance on the trail with an injured arm and a weighted backpack. She stared him straight in the eye until he backed down and turned away.

He stalked toward the mouth of the cave without looking back. "I'm going to make sure no one is outside or waiting up the trail."

She'd wounded his pride, but there was nothing that could be done about it. Whether he admitted it or not, he knew she was right.

When she hitched the backpack onto her shoulders, every muscle screamed that she had not slept in a nice soft bed last night… Oh, and that she'd battled a blazing inferno only twelve hours earlier.

Only twelve hours?

Lord, let twelve more hours bring the end of this whole ordeal. Please.

"It's clear. Let's go."

She slipped out of the cave, her eyes burning in the morning light. The sun had barely crept over the horizon, the sky a blaze of orange and pink, but it was too much for her cave-darkened vision to handle. Wincing, she shut her eyes then opened them slowly, hoping to ease them into reality.

"They should have put sunglasses in this backpack." She instantly regretted mumbling the complaint. The canvas bag she'd slung over her shoulders had probably saved their lives. If she died today, it wouldn't be from too much sun in her eyes.

She really needed another line of thinking.

Falling in behind Jacob, she let him set the pace. His body had endured more than hers.

Behind them, the canyon opened up, wide and deep, a masterpiece of art in the rising sunlight. Before them, the winding trail hugged the rock face, the canyon narrowing as it reached into the distance.

It was tough going and silent between them as they hiked their way up, the trail sometimes steep and often narrow. More than once, she hugged the rock wall and said a prayer of thanks that they hadn't tumbled down in their night-darkened flight. She couldn't see how they'd survived.

Forcing her mind off what could have happened, Ivy focused on the present. Her feet ached in running shoes that were never intended for hiking. Every step jarred a muscle somewhere in her body. Even her jaw hurt. They hadn't been on the trail for ten minutes before she'd gritted her back teeth, forcing every step by sheer willpower, keeping the image of her daughter before her.

She had to survive for Wren. And the only way to survive was to keep putting one foot in front of the other.

They'd been hiking about an hour when Jacob suddenly stopped.

Her mind lulled into numbness, Ivy walked right into him. Immediately, she ducked closer to the rock face, certain he'd spotted danger on the trail.

"There's nobody coming, but we've got more immediate problems." Jacob stepped to the side so she could see what was in front of him.

At some point during the night, the land on the rim had given way, probably loosened by the driving rainstorm that had ripped violently through during the afternoon.

A rock slide had tumbled down the canyon wall, taking the narrow trail with it. There was nothing left, only a hole twenty feet across that plunged into nothingness.

Their only way out had been obliterated.

FOURTEEN

In his entire life, there had never been a moment when Jacob truly wanted to give up. Not when his father had passed away. Not when he'd walked away from Ivy. Not even when he'd awakened in a medical facility with his internal organs in shambles and his future in doubt.

There had been days when sheer stubborn willpower and prayer had been the only things that had carried him through multiple surgeries and physical therapy. When only the determination to not be lost for the rest of his life had pushed him through the physical tests he'd had to pass to take on his investigative job with the National Park Service.

But this might be what finally broke him.

Their escape route was destroyed. They were both physically and mentally exhausted. He'd taken inventory of their supplies while Ivy slept this morning. They'd barely had enough provisions for this shorter hike. If they had to take another route, it would take days. At that point, lack of food would be a nonissue, because their meager supply of water combined with their weakened physical condition would bring death before they could ever starve.

At best, they had a day before their bodies abandoned the fight.

Ivy backed away from the destroyed trail and dropped onto a boulder, burying her face in her hands.

He'd give her a minute. The way his mind was spinning, he didn't want anyone to speak to him, either. It would take a second to switch gears and fully absorb the situation.

Edging as close to the washed-out trail as he dared, he looked over the edge. Climbing down and back up again would be impossible. And there was no ledge left for them to creep along to the other side.

His mind and body begged him to sit and rest, but if he did, he'd never get up again. Instead, he paced a few feet back the way they'd come and stared into the distance. The canyon sprawled before him, the shadows of night finally giving way to the sun as it made its way high enough to peek over the rim.

They were a few miles past the edge of his family's land. While he'd hiked to the cave countless times, he'd never gone past it. The route was strenuous as the land dropped about a thousand feet over the course of a mile. It wasn't technically even a route. It was a trek through the backcountry, a steep hike down into a primitive area of the canyon with no cultivated trail.

The upside was that it eventually led to an unnamed creek that should be running, given the rain they'd had over the last few days. All that did was solve their water problems…sort of. They had matches and could boil water in the canteen, but that would only yield a little bit at a time.

It would have to be enough.

He had no idea what lay past that. It was possible they

could follow the creek to the Colorado River and a beach, where some rafters could be overnighting.

It was also possible they could pick their way down that steep incline and along the creek only to wind up on a bluff over the river with no way down and a body-destroying climb back up.

There was one more option that he wasn't certain was actually an option. Somewhere along one of the branches of that creek, a primitive trail led to the Tonto Trail. While it was a known, mapped route, the Tonto was long and winding, running roughly parallel to and above the Colorado River. It eventually led to other trails and civilization, but there were a lot of hard, rough miles along the way.

He'd hiked the Tonto from Bright Angel to the South Kaibab a few times, but that was on the more heavily traveled section of the trail to the west of their location. This early in the spring, there wouldn't be a lot of traffic this far east, and the trail would be overgrown in spots. Even if they were in peak physical condition, the climbs and descents would quickly wear on them. They'd also be in danger of wandering into a situation where they were hopelessly lost.

No map. No equipment. No supplies. He'd never been in a situation with less hope.

With every moment that passed, they were more likely to die in the Grand Canyon, only a handful of miles yet light-years from civilization. They'd leave their daughter an orphan who might never know what happened to her parents.

And it was his fault. He'd missed so many signs. Made so many wrong choices.

"We'll stay here." Ivy's voice cut through his futile planning session.

When he turned, she was standing between him and the massive gash in the trail that might be the end of them. She'd drawn back her shoulders and was standing as tall as he'd ever seen her.

But her face was pale and her hands were shaking. There was a limit to what willpower could do.

He paced a few careful steps toward her. "Stay here?"

"The ambulance is still up there. Angie knows this trail is here. Sooner or later, she'll make sure someone directs searchers this way. They can figure out how to reach us."

She was right. They'd discussed that very thing earlier, but in his frustration and exhaustion, the facts had deserted him. In his haste to find a way out, he'd forgotten to fully evaluate the situation. Again. It seemed he'd never learn.

"I have some lovely seating options while you wait for your party to arrive." Ivy gestured toward the rock she'd been sitting on earlier, her smile forced. She was choosing to make the best of a situation that literally couldn't get any worse. "We can discuss the weather. Or the delightful food choices on our lunch menu, which will be available in a few hours. You can dine on a chilled energy bar or, if you prefer, I can lay one in the sun and you can sample our lukewarm option."

In spite of everything, Jacob laughed. It was no wonder he loved this woman. And he did love her.

He just couldn't tell her, not while they were in danger and even survival was so uncertain. And certainly not while fear ruled her life. It wouldn't be fair.

Jacob scratched his chin, playing along and pretending to think. "Right now, I'll try the seating, but I think I'd like to be farther down the trail, away from the giant hole in your floor."

"As you wish." Ivy walked to a bend in the trail and sat with her back against the rock face.

Joining her, Jacob turned his face to the sky, letting the sun warm his body. Hopefully, it would ease some of the pain in his joints. It had been a while since everything hurt all at the same time. "Was there any sunscreen in that pack?"

"Not that I saw."

They'd have to find shade soon, but for now, he was oddly content to sit in the awakening day and wait. To their right, the trail wound back toward where they'd left the ambulance, the path eventually leading into the trees as it angled up to the ravine. To their left, the path curved and disappeared around the rock face. From their vantage point, the vastness of the canyon spread before them, harsh yet beautiful.

The morning sun painted the canyon in brilliant shades of orange, red and brown. There were even green patches in the higher elevations and along hidden springs and creeks. It really was a *wonder*.

Jacob had done countless day hikes and a dozen longer hikes in his lifetime. But this time… "You know, I never really sit still and take the time to just look." When he was on the trail, he charged from one point to the next, not really stopping to take in what was going on around him. Sort of like his life.

"I guess when you grow up with it in your backyard, you sort of take it for granted."

He lifted his good shoulder in a shrug. She could be right. But when he got out of here, he intended to slow down. To lift his head from his work and look around. To convince Ivy that their family was worth risking everything to build.

They might as well have that conversation now. It wasn't like they were going anywhere in a hurry. She sure couldn't get up and walk out if she didn't like the direction he headed. "Can we talk about something?"

Although Ivy wasn't touching him, he could sense her posture stiffening. Maybe she wasn't ready to hear it, but he was ready to say it.

He wanted to try again. And that kiss in his kitchen made him believe she did, too. She still trusted him, still wanted him. He just needed to prove it to her. "What made you come to me for help?"

"Jacob." She shook her head and leaned forward as if what she had to say carried weight. "I'm not—"

Rock exploded above her head. The crack of a rifle shot echoed and re-echoed.

Ivy screamed.

What...?

Ivy froze. Her lungs refused to inhale. Her mind froze.

"Move!" Jacob pulled her to her feet, shoving her ahead of him around the bend in the trail.

Another blast shattered the rock where she'd been sitting. That was gunfire.

Gunfire?

Her feet found traction, and she raced around the trail bend with Jacob as another shot shattered the rock by her head.

Dust and dirt coated her eyes. She stumbled ahead of Jacob. Shelter. They needed shelter. But the cave was a mile away. They'd never make it.

"Stop." Jacob grabbed the back of her shirt and pulled her to a stop. "Ivy, stop. They can't hit us from here. There's too much of a turn in the trail. We're sheltered."

Backing against the rock, Ivy dropped the pack she'd instinctively grabbed. She doubled over, pressing her hands to her knees. If there had been anything in her stomach, it might not have stayed there. "What...happened?" She straightened to look past Jacob, back up the trail. She'd imagined that, right?

Taking up a position beside her, Jacob tilted his head and stared at the sky, shoulders rising and falling as he heaved air in and out. "I don't know."

That wasn't true. Both of them knew what neither wanted to acknowledge. Their pursuers had come back. The only thing standing between them and death was the destroyed trail.

With one last deep breath, Jacob turned toward her. "They can't get over that gap in the trail. They'll have to find another way around. We have some time to figure out what to do."

"Cave?" Bracing against her knees, Ivy stood straight. Their only safe space was the dark hole they'd emerged from less than two hours earlier.

Jacob stared into the distance, but it was obvious he didn't see the broad canyon. He was calculating. Finally, he shook his head slowly, his expression grim and tight. "No."

"No?" They literally had nowhere else to go. "Rescue can't find us if we get too far from the trail."

"And if that shooter finds a way in first, we're trapped between them and the washout." Jacob dragged his good hand down his face, where a beard had shadowed it. "We have to head down into the canyon."

Away from help. Away from rescue.

Away from Wren.

Ivy closed her eyes against an onslaught of tears that threatened to burst through her defenses. When they'd set out this morning, she'd believed they'd be almost back to safety by now. That she was only a couple of hours away from a reunion with her daughter.

Now? Nothing was certain. She might never get out of the canyon.

Jacob wanted to plunge deeper into an unknown that was already terrifying. He hadn't said it, but she'd hiked with him enough to know their situation was dire. When they'd made day treks into the canyon in college, his entire family had emphasized the need to stay hydrated and to fuel up with high-calorie meals and snacks.

They had none of that. And they'd been weak before they started.

She also knew the condition of the trail below the cave entrance. Jacob had once told her it was steep and difficult to navigate. They'd never make it. She turned to reason with him, but he was already watching her.

"I know." His voice was low and weighted with more emotion than she wanted to acknowledge, as though the gravity of their situation had pulled the words to the ground. "But we don't know if Sienna Davies has already sent part of her team up from the other side. They could already be on the move, could pin us in before rescue can get here." He chewed his lower lip and studied the horizon. "It could take a day or so for them to get here, but…"

But just when Ivy had thought it couldn't get any worse, it had.

Everything in her body felt like it was going to slide down into the canyon. Her muscles, her lungs, her head…

They all ached with various degrees of intensity. Even her thoughts were heavy. It was all enough to drag her to the ground, never to get up again.

She might as well quit. They were never going to win.

"Ivy." Jacob reached for her hand and tugged her gently to him. He wrapped his arm around her waist and pulled her close to his side. "We're going to make it."

"You don't know that." The tone of her voice sounded like Wren in full pout. It was a pathetic whine and she hated it, but she lacked the willpower to care. "Our choices stink. We can sit and wait for them to kill us, or we can wander around in some of the most brutal territory on earth until—"

"Or..." The word held enough force to silence her pitiful tirade. He pressed a kiss to her temple and lowered his mouth to her ear, then whispered, "Or we can get out of here alive and get home to our daughter."

Our daughter. Wren. They would both get home for Wren.

And maybe for them.

For several heartbeats, she rested in his embrace, drawing on his strength. Eventually she pulled away and moved her hair off her forehead. "Let's go before that shooter figures out how to pole vault."

With a tight smile that was definitely fake, Jacob saluted her and swept his hand forward. "After you."

Ivy turned and headed down the trail. This was not a path she'd ever imagined she'd walk, but she intended to get back to her daughter...or give her last breath trying.

FIFTEEN

The air in the canyon was hot and still. Although the highs on the rim rarely got above the seventies this time of year, below the rim, the air grew warmer and heavier the farther they descended. The chill from the previous day's front was a memory by midday. By the time they'd picked their way down the steep grade to level land approaching the creek, they were sweating, losing more precious water by the second.

Jacob was light-headed and dizzy. Heat cramps and every other kind of pain were taking a toll and muddling his thoughts. He could see their destination in the near distance, less than half a mile away, but by this point, he wasn't certain it wasn't a mirage.

In front of him, Ivy had slowed considerably during the descent. She was picking her way down, but Jacob was sure she was suffering from the same head-swimming vertigo that afflicted him. Exertion, dehydration and hunger were wicked foes individually. Blended together, they were toxic.

It had been over an hour since they'd stopped for water and an energy bar. The four ounces in the pouch hadn't been nearly enough, and they were down to two each. If they couldn't light a fire and boil water in that canteen soon, they'd be out of chances.

When they stepped into the shade of a handful of juniper trees at a curve in the stream, Ivy dropped to her knees and shed the backpack. Her face was pale beneath a sunburn, and her eyes were red from dust, heat and unfiltered sunlight. "If I'm dreaming we made it, don't wake me." Her voice was raw and scratchy. "I'm about to lie down in that water."

"It wouldn't do you much good." Even with recent rain, the creek was only running about two feet wide and a couple of inches deep. It had been too dry and there hadn't been enough snow for any of the waterways to run wild, though this one obviously had at one time. Only a few meters from their oasis, it dropped several stories over the edge into a narrow slot that had seen plenty of water in the past. Beyond that, the canyon opened up. If he remembered his map correctly, this was the last water for some time.

He squatted on shaky legs and studied the water. It would be silty. He'd have to strain it through gauze into the canteen. Even boiled it would taste like metal, dirt and minerals, but he doubted either of them would notice. "As soon as I get a fire going, we'll drink the last of the emergency water."

Ivy nodded, then rolled onto her back and stared at the sky. "I'll help you gather wood in a minute."

"No need." She'd already dropped. If she was able to get up anytime soon, he'd be surprised. It would take all he had to gather dry twigs and break off a few limbs. Hopefully, he could get a fire good enough to boil water.

He didn't want to consider what would happen if he failed.

He also didn't want to consider what would happen if Sienna Davies or her cohorts spotted smoke. He could only fight one battle at a time, and the first was to get them hydrated.

By the time he'd managed a small fire, he was more than ready to suck down another four-ounce water pouch. Ivy had found her second wind—although they were both way past their third and fourth—and had moved to sit by him as he filtered water through the gauze, then set the canteen near the flames to let the heat do its work.

"How do you plan to get it out of there once it's hot?" Ivy settled against a tree and stared into the flames. She'd splashed water on her face, and wet tendrils hung along one cheek.

"I'll cross that bridge when I come to it."

"Doesn't sound any different than how we've rolled all along. Winging it." She took the sting out of the words with a smile. "Know what I can't wait for? A shower. And a toothbrush."

"I felt that all the way to my gut." Jacob slid over and sat on the side of the tree at a right angle to her, their shoulders touching.

She handed him the pouch of water. Tapping hers against his in salute, she tore it open and sipped it.

He did the same. The warm water hit his tongue and it was tough not to guzzle. He let it sit for a few seconds, wetting his dry mouth before he swallowed. He could feel it along every inch of his throat. "Actually, I'm ready for a tall glass of iced tea, dripping condensation along—"

"Stop." Ivy elbowed him in the side. "Some things are just mean."

He ducked away and chuckled. It was a good thing she was on the side of his good arm.

They sat in silence until Ivy relaxed and her breathing dropped into a regular rhythm. At least she was sleeping. He was pretty sure she hadn't gotten much rest overnight. Every time he'd jolted awake, she'd already been alert.

When the water in the canteen started to boil, he counted to six hundred, hoping that had gotten him over five minutes. With a stick, he dragged the canteen away from the heat and banked the fire so they could restart it if necessary that night. It would likely get down into the forties, and they had no shelter other than the trees and their survival blankets.

Jacob crept back to the tree and sat against it. He let his mind wander, trying to calculate how long it would take Sienna Davies to make her way to them. Even if she'd left last night, which she likely hadn't, they were more than a day's hike in. Her potshots at them this morning said they had a head start on her.

He scanned the open view of the canyon on the other side of the trees that clustered around the creek. There was no sign of civilization, not even a trail. Without a compass, he had no way to truly navigate past the inexact use of the sun. He'd studied the canyon. Had grown up near this section, but he knew it was primitive. Civilization was a couple of days away and a steep hike up.

He closed his dry, scratchy eyes. *I don't see a way out of here, God. But You've got the bird's-eye view...*

A sudden sharp pain in his hip jolted him out of a sleep he hadn't even realized he'd tumbled into. Jerking awake, he reached out with his good hand and tried to brace himself to stand, but another blow had him leaning forward for protection.

What was happening?

He squeezed his eyes shut against the pain and the

light that blazed between the trees. When he opened them, he was staring at a pair of gray hiking boots.

A shadow blocked the sun.

A man's voice dropped on him like a crushing rock slide. "Well, Special Agent Garcia. You just made me a very rich man."

Jacob's vision cleared and he immediately wished it hadn't.

He was literally staring down the barrel of a gun only a couple feet from his face. His heart kick-started against his rib cage, the adrenaline surge a painful reminder that everything in his body was already depleted and hurting.

He couldn't focus on that now. Instead, he forced himself to steady his breathing. To not show fear. To tear his focus from the gun, up the arm...

To a face he recognized.

His voice had better not betray his dehydration and exhaustion. He took a second to gather the name in his throat before he attempted to speak. It needed force. The authority of his position with the National Park Service. He hardened his expression. "Daniel Adams."

The National Park Service's most-wanted artifact poacher sneered down at Jacob, his blue eyes cold.

But how? How had the man his team had been hunting for months managed to stumble on them while they were running from a contract killer?

There's no such thing as coincidence. He'd learned it well as a military police officer and as an investigator.

Jacob nodded slowly as the pieces fell into place. "Sienna Davies hired you because you know the canyon." It made perfect sense. Rather than chance the hike into rugged and dangerous territory herself, she'd managed to contact one of the most well-known, fiercely hunted artifact smugglers in the country. "How?" Nothing in their intel on Adams indicated a link to the hired gun.

Adams merely arched an eyebrow, as though he was mildly impressed Jacob had figured him out. "We make our money where we can."

"And you know who I am."

"It pays to know the team that's hunting you. Helps you stay one step ahead. I watch. I listen. I've seen you in action." He shrugged. "You're smart, Special Agent Garcia. But somehow, you missed me."

With a groan, Ivy stirred beside him. Her shoulder brushed his. They were sitting too close to one another, were emotionally leaning too much on each other, and that would never work given the change in their situation. The very last thing he needed was for a man like Daniel Adams to realize there was more than a professional connection between the two of them. He'd exploit that to get what he wanted.

Because it was clear he wanted something. If he didn't, they'd have both been shot at point-blank range in their sleep. From all he'd read on Adams, the man was ruthless and greedy, grasping for money wherever he could get it and, currently, he was getting it in black-market artifact sales. He wasn't typically a killer, though, so they might have some time to get out of this.

He just had to clear his head and figure out how.

And keep Ivy from revealing to their captor that they were linked by anything more than an investigation.

That meant asserting control, just like he would if this was any other case she was a part of. He slapped the back of his hand against her leg. "Bridges. Wake up.

We have company." Maybe she'd catch on to the use of her last name.

It was a thin thread to hitch their lives on, but he had to grasp for whatever he could.

He shoved his shoulder against hers. "I said we've got company."

With a start, Ivy scrambled to her feet, probably startled by the rude awakening. She pressed tighter against the tree and nearly ducked behind it, her eyes glued to the gun that Adams had swung in her direction.

Anger surged through Jacob's system, hot beneath his already heated skin. The direct threat to Ivy was more than he could handle. It took everything Jacob had not to leap at the man, but a physical assault would be deadly in his current weakened condition. He didn't have enough strength left for a fight.

There had to be another way.

"Who are you?" Ivy's voice shook, cracking under the strain of their situation and her dehydration, but it was firm.

"Ask your bodyguard." Keeping the gun trained, Adams backed up a couple of steps and reached down to pull the canteen from where Jacob had left it to cool. He passed it to Ivy. "Drink this."

Right there. That was what would save them.

Jacob clamped down on the inside of his lip to keep from letting a grin slip through. Adams had a weakness. A soft spot. Jacob knew from his file that he'd been raised by his mother and grandmother, and that he had three sisters. Clearly, something of a gentleman lived inside the criminal, at least enough of one to prevent him from watching a woman suffer needlessly.

Even one who had a price on her head.

Ivy stared at the canteen, but she didn't reach for it. Instead, she stood with her hands behind her back, seeming to size up the man in front of her. Her head tilted. Her eyes narrowed.

To anyone who didn't know her, it would look like she was waking up. Jacob knew better. She was thinking. Plotting. The set to her jaw was as familiar as his own face in the mirror.

Don't be stubborn and refuse water, Ivy. He wanted to tug at her jeans and nudge her forward. She needed it. She dare not turn away from it in some rebellious, take-a-stand refusal.

She shook her head slowly and pointed at Jacob. "He drinks first."

What was she doing? Why was she singling him out? He tried not to tense. *Ivy, don't let him know we have a history. Possibly a future.*

"He's injured. And I'm not taking in anything until he's taken care of."

Jacob's pride bucked. He bristled at her frank declaration of his weakness to his enemy. He'd gotten them into this. Had injured himself in the process of saving them. Now she was pointing out his failings to the man who held their lives in his hands. To a man who needed to think he was strong—

Except maybe he didn't.

Way to go, Ivy. Balling his fist at his side, Jacob fought the urge to cheer. The woman was a genius. She'd sized up Daniel Adams. Had deduced the same thing Jacob had—that soft spot for a female.

The weaker she made Jacob appear, the more Adams would dismiss and underestimate him.

Adams eyed her, annoyance twitching his cheek. Finally, he shrugged and shook the canteen at Ivy. "Fine. Whatever."

Ivy grabbed the canteen quickly and backed away as though she feared what Adams would do to her if she let him get too close. She was scared, no doubt, but she was also acting more afraid than she probably was. She shrunk from no one. Her father had cautioned her against letting anyone smell fear. If she was cowering, there was a calculated reason.

She'd better know what she was doing.

Because if Daniel Adams was playing gun-for-hire to Sienna Davies, one misstep would get them both killed.

SIXTEEN

Jacob had better realize she had picked up on his signals. She'd pegged this guy the instant he'd held out the canteen to her.

There was no doubt he was capable of killing. His casual handling of that pistol said more than she wanted to hear. And he wouldn't hesitate to pull the trigger, if he was angered.

But if he was pushed just far enough, he'd lose his temper and make a mistake. The key to that temper was Ivy. He clearly had a soft spot for her. Probably for all women. She'd seen it in the courtroom waiting on hearings, watching other cases presented before Judge Kenneth Mitchell. He tried to be impartial, but he somehow always seemed to treat females more gently than males. He'd been raised by a mother who sacrificed to raise him, who'd needed care in later life when she'd been diagnosed with multiple sclerosis. There was always something about the concern in his eyes.

Of course, she'd seen the opposite as well. Men who hated women simply because they were women. But whatever had turned this guy to crime, it wasn't hatred of females.

Even though he had a gun trained on her, she saw the same kind of concern Judge Mitchell carried in this man's expression. Oh, there was no doubt he'd kill her if he got the order, but he wouldn't take pleasure in doing it. He knew her death warrant had been signed, but he didn't act like he would cause her undue suffering.

The thought of this man showing her compassion while he played a part in her murder squiggled her already raging stomach. But that compassion was going to work to their advantage.

She had the distinct feeling, as Jacob drained the canteen, that he was going to see just how far he could push their captor, who was glaring at him as though he wished he could pull the trigger.

"What are you doing?" Without warning, Adams turned the gun on Jacob, his voice ragged with anger. "Give her the water."

With a sheepish look, Jacob lowered the canteen from his lips then turned it upside down.

It was empty.

"Look, Adams, I didn't realize how much I was drinking." He looked up at Ivy and his tone changed. "I'm sorry."

Adams spat a string of words that should have left the surrounding canyon dripping in blue.

Ivy's heart beat faster, and she dug her fingers into the bark of the juniper tree. She wavered on her feet, dizzy and craving the water Jacob had just guzzled.

He'd better know what he was doing, and it needed to work. Building sympathy for her at the expense of his own safety could backfire quickly.

Adams whipped the gun to aim at Jacob and stalked

closer, but he stopped just out of reach. His finger tightened on the trigger as his expression flamed with anger.

Ivy's voice stuck in her throat. She wanted to cry out.
To scream at him not to do this, but the words wouldn't
work their way past the pressure in her throat and the
desert in her mouth.

With another impressive display of vocabulary, Adams
lowered the pistol and backed past their campfire.

It was all Ivy could do not to drop to the ground and
throw her arms around Jacob. To somehow shield him
from the wrath that was probably headed his way. But
the way he'd awakened her so roughly and had called her
"Bridges," she knew he wanted Adams to believe there
was nothing personal between them.

It was going to kill her to keep her distance.

Her knees gave out as her adrenaline ebbed, and she
sank to the ground, using the tree for support. She leaned
her shoulder against the bark and tried not to put herself
right out in the dirt and rock.

Across the campfire, Adams dug through a backpack
with one hand while he kept the gun trained on them
with the other. He returned, tossing a can of water to
Ivy. "Here."

His shirt shifted as he moved, revealing a satellite
phone at his waist.

A sat phone would be their salvation. If only she could
grab it. It was so close, so achingly close.

And so far away. She fumbled the can and had to retrieve it when it rolled toward Jacob. It was slightly cool
to the touch. The water inside wasn't quite lukewarm.
It felt even cooler than it probably was to her hot, dry
mouth. Wherever Adams had come from, it couldn't have

been very far. Somewhere nearby there was some form of civilization.

Or there was a literal den of thieves camping out in the canyon.

Nausea rocked her as the water hit her stomach. She slowed down, trying to sip instead of gulp.

Within minutes—long minutes of silence, where Davis glared at Jacob and Jacob glared back—something like strength washed over Ivy. She was still gut-level hungry, but her body absorbed the water with gusto.

Maybe Jacob was feeling the same.

"Got any food?" Jacob jerked his chin at their captor. "It's been a while."

"For her? Sure," Adams sneered at him and went to the backpack again.

When their foe glanced down into it, Jacob whispered, "Follow my lead."

Oh, how she wanted to argue. Whatever he was about to do, it was going to be dangerous for them. It was clear that Adams was under some sort of directive to keep them alive, probably until Sienna Davies could arrive and finish the job herself, but he'd also likely get some percentage of his blood money even if they weren't breathing when she came on the scene.

When Adams returned, he tossed a pack of freeze-dried food toward Ivy.

Before she could react, Jacob's good arm reached across her and caught the food. He eyed Adams defiantly. "Now get her one."

With a roar, he snapped the weapon higher, aimed at Jacob's head. "That's it, Garcia."

Ivy choked back a scream, and it leaked out as a whimper.

Neither of the men seemed to notice. They were too intent on staring each other down.

Jacob spoke first. "You won't kill me. Davies wants us alive. If she didn't, we'd already be dead. You only get paid if you deliver us breathing."

That seemed to enrage Adams even more. His face reddened. His shoulders heaved. "She has questions. Wants you alive." Shoving the gun into the back of his waistband, he stalked closer to Jacob. "That doesn't mean you can't be almost dead when she gets here."

"No." Ivy's shout came out as a ragged whisper that Adams ignored as he advanced.

Adams stalked to Jacob and pulled back his leg to deliver a blow to Jacob's ribs. If he landed that blow just right, the internal damage would kill him.

Lord, help me. Jacob only had one shot, and it had better connect.

Jacob threw one leg up and around, catching Adams in the knee. He hopped sideways, lost his footing, dropped then rolled to all fours. Before he could recover, Jacob was on his feet, delivering his own swift kick to the other man's ribs instead.

Adams jerked and howled, burying his face in the ground and instinctively wrapping his arms around his chest.

Ivy jumped up.

"Stay back!" He didn't need her in the middle of the fray. If Adams grabbed her, any orders Sienna Davies had handed him would no longer matter. He'd kill them both and deal with her wrath in the aftermath.

She hesitated then backed away. Hopefully, she'd stay there.

Jacobs circled slightly out of Adams's reach, evaluating the situation. If he got to his feet, there'd be no way to fight him one-armed. He had to keep the other man down.

As Adams shook his head and struggled to rise, Jacob brought the heel of his boot down on the small of his back, driving him to the ground.

Leaving the gun he'd tucked into his waistband exposed.

Jacob swooped in and pulled the pistol free. He backed away and leveled the weapon at center mass just as Adams managed to roll onto his back.

Huffing, Adams eyed Jacob, his gaze glittering with pain and calculation.

"I wouldn't move too fast." Jacob backed away another step, keeping the weapon trained on Adams's chest. "I'm not under any orders from Sienna Davies to keep you alive." He hated making threats, but it was the only language a guy like Adams spoke.

Well, that and cold cash. Jacob was in short supply of that.

Adams tightened his jaw and stared at Jacob. If he could kill with a look, Jacob would have been vaporized and Ivy would be left to fend for herself.

Now, what to do with Adams? They had no restraints, and he couldn't guard an angry prisoner indefinitely.

This kept getting worse. He needed time. And answers. "Why does Davies want to keep us alive? You could have just killed us and collected the cash."

Adams glanced at Ivy, who was several feet away, still standing by the tree, but his eyes quickly came back to the gun Jacob had trained on him. "She wants to know what you've seen and who you've told."

Well, he certainly wasn't going to hand out that information, especially not when it was the only reason both of them were still breathing. Daniel Adams might be answering to Sienna Davies, but Sienna Davies ultimately answered to Ross Evans. The judge was the man calling the shots, the one who had everything to lose. He couldn't risk loose ends and would want to know everything Jacob and Ivy knew.

As long as Sienna Davies was unsure who knew what, Jacob and Ivy would remain alive.

Although she might resort to torture to get the intel she needed.

Jacob almost gagged at the thought of Ivy in a ruthless killer's hands, but he swallowed hard. *One fight at a time.* "What else?"

"Look, I don't know her. We don't move in the same circles." Breathing heavily and grimacing against the pain, Daniel Adams pushed up onto his elbows. "She put out a general call over satellite radio. Anybody in the vicinity carrying one heard it. If there are any more guys out here like me, then they're looking for you, too. I spotted the smoke from your fire. Radioed the coordinates back to her and came to make sure you didn't move." His smile was disgusting. "And to collect my money when she shows."

"So you weren't that far away." If he could get out of here with that kind of intel from Adams, they might be able to bust up his entire ring.

"Nice try. I'm not giving up where my crew is digging." Smirking, Adams shook his head. "Not that it matters. Davies is headed this way. Should be here within the hour, given her connections." He winced as he eased up to a sitting position, digging his fingers into the dirt and fighting for balance. "She'll pay me and handle you."

"She'll kill all of us." Ivy spoke up from her position near the tree. "She has no reason to keep you alive."

The triumphant grin Adams had been wearing faltered, but only for a second. "That saying? 'Honor among thieves?' I haven't ever seen it fail."

Jacob glanced at Ivy and shook his head. "There's a first time for—" Gravel and dirt hit him in the eye.

Blinking, he staggered back two steps, struggling to keep from dropping the pistol to tend to his face.

Ivy screamed.

When his eyes cleared, Adams was standing.

He had Ivy in front of him, his arm wrapped tightly around her throat. Gone was any sympathy for her. All the man wanted was to save his own skin. "I'll break her neck. Lay down the pistol and back away."

It took everything in Jacob not to charge. His fingers flexed and relaxed on the pistol grip, then tightened again. He'd been trained to never surrender his weapon under any circumstances.

He'd never once imagined that "any circumstances" would include a threat to the woman he loved.

Adams jerked Ivy around to his front and she winced at the rough treatment, her eyes wide and pinned on Jacob's.

This time, there was no hiding her fear. She struggled, her face turning a sick shade of purple as Adams tightened his grip.

He backed another step away from Jacob, his hiking boots splashing in the shallow creek. He was too close to the ledge, increasing the threat to Ivy's life. If he went over... "All I have to do is wait you out. Davies will take care of you when she gets here."

He was right, to a point. Davies would arrive, but she had no idea Jacob was armed. It was a point in his favor.

But it didn't rescue Ivy.

Her fight became more feeble, and she slowly stopped struggling. Suddenly, her body went limp, the deadweight dragging Adams forward a half step.

Adams struggled to hold her up, his expression shifting from conceit to shock. He'd gone too far.

Her foot caught between two rocks and her leg twisted as she slipped from his grasp and melted into the shallow stream.

Too late, Jacob pulled his gaze from Ivy's still form.

Adams charged.

Jacob took aim and squeezed the trigger.

Immediately, a red stain appeared at Adams's shoulder. He staggered back, his eyes wide with shock and pain. Another step. His heel caught Ivy's hip behind him, and he flailed, trying to regain his footing.

Jacob raced forward, but he wasn't quick enough.

Adams disappeared over the edge.

SEVENTEEN

"Ivy."

Her name came from somewhere above her. Through a long tunnel.

"Ivy." Louder this time. More frantic. In Jacob's voice.

Jacob's panicked voice.

Shuddering against her body's desire to stay asleep, Ivy shuddered and inhaled deeply, her throat aching worse than ever.

Her throat. That man's arm around her throat. The world growing darker.

Gasping, Ivy opened her eyes and sat up suddenly. She was wet from the stream. Her ankle throbbed. And she was in Jacob's arms. "Jacob?"

"It's okay. He's gone."

Where? How?

Actually, answers could wait. Somehow, she was safe.

Turning in Jacob's embrace, she buried her face in his shoulder and finally wept. She'd bucked up and swallowed fear as long as she could. Now, scared and hungry and physically depleted, she had nothing left to fight with. Another man had tried to kill her. A murderer was headed their way. And they were still lost in the Grand

Canyon. Her sobs were dry and heaving. She didn't even have enough water in her body to make tears.

And that made everything worse.

Jacob let her cry, his hand making circles on her back. He said nothing, just held her.

It shouldn't have felt safe, but somehow, it did. Still, their situation hadn't changed. They were still straddling the line between life and death.

But they were together. Easing away from him, she pressed dry, hot fingers to scratchy, hot eyes. "What happened?"

Jacob glanced behind her. "He went over the edge."

When she scrambled to turn and look behind her, he grasped her chin and gently turned her to the front. "Don't. You don't want to look."

No, she didn't. Her imagination was bad enough. "Now what?"

"Well, it sounds mercenary but…" Jacob stood and held out his hand to help Ivy up. "We should eat."

The backpack. That man, Adams, had pulled food and water out of his trail pack. With a grateful glance at Jacob, Ivy grasped his hand and slid her feet under her to stand.

Her right ankle shuddered under a lightning bolt of pain, dropping her into the water again.

Jacob stumbled trying to catch her and went down to one knee in the stream, wincing as he hit. "Ivy. What's wrong?"

"I don't know." Reaching down, she felt her ankle. It was throbbing, hot and twice as big as it should be. This was bad. Really bad.

And from the look on Jacob's face, he was coming to that realization as well. He was battling a potential fracture. She was hobbled by what was either a sprained ankle or a broken bone.

There would be no more hiking.

Jacob edged to her foot and gently assessed her ankle, his expression tight. When he sat back on his heels, he rubbed at his knee absently and stared at her foot as though wishing he could change the situation with sheer hope. "Wait." The hope he was waiting for seemed to bloom on his face. "A sat phone. Adams said that Sienna Davies sent out a—"

"I saw it earlier. It was on his belt. If he's over the edge, it went with him." That was it then. They had truly run out of ways to escape.

Jacob seemed to deflate, his shoulders slumping and his chin dipping to his chest. Either he'd given up completely or he was praying.

That's what she should be doing, but at the moment, she couldn't muster the energy to even talk to God. Too many prayers had already been shattered. She couldn't figure out what He was doing. All Ivy knew was she didn't like any of it.

Jacob pulled back his shoulders, then shook his head, stood and helped her up. Together, they hobbled to the tree where they'd slept earlier, and she settled to the ground. Still silent, he propped her foot up on the backpack that had been their faithful friend on this flight, then grabbed Adams's backpack and settled beside her.

He dumped the contents on the ground—a handheld GPS and map that would have brought elation earlier, but were useless to them in her condition. Two more cans of water. A purification kit. Energy bars. And several packs of freeze-dried food.

"At least we can eat for a couple of days." Jacob held

up two of the packs. "Pad Thai or fettuccine Alfredo?" He was clearly trying to make the best of it.

Something Ivy wasn't sure she wanted to do. "You should go without me. Get help. Bring back—"

"No." He went to the fire and stoked it, then dropped some more sticks on it. "I'll boil more water and we'll eat, then we'll—"

"Nothing else makes sense. Leave me the energy bars and water. Take the rest of the food with—"

"I said no." When he faced her, his expression was stormy. "Have you forgotten that Sienna Davies is headed to this location? She'll get here before I can even get packed. This is it, Ivy. We eat, then we defend ourselves."

Their last stand.

Her head started to pound in a whole new way. A rhythmic whomping that seemed to start in her ears and assaulted her from the outside in. So many things had been unbearable, but this roar out of the silence was almost enough to make her head explode.

Wait. A roar from the silence.

Ivy grabbed the tree, braced on her good leg and got to her feet. She stared at Jacob, who was watching her with wide eyes. What was that sound? It was familiar… Something she'd heard before…

The pounding grew louder.

Jacob dropped everything and ran out from under the shade of the tree, looking up.

The roar grew deafening, and a shadow raced along the ground. A black, white and yellow National Park Service helicopter appeared over the wall of the canyon they had picked their way down and hovered overhead.

Sliding to the ground, Ivy buried her face in her hands. They were saved.

* * *

"Where's Ivy?" Sitting on the edge of the hospital bed, Jacob eyed Linc, who was leaning against the wall by the door with his arms crossed over his chest.

Jacob held his arm out straight while a nurse reattached his IV line after they'd finally given in and let him have a shower. Clean and dressed in the sweats Linc had brought, he felt more human.

But he wouldn't feel alive until someone told him how Ivy was.

It had been hours since they'd been airlifted to the hospital in Flagstaff. Hours without seeing for himself that she was safe. He was two seconds from dragging his IV pole around the building until he found her.

Linc grinned that knowing grin that always infuriated Jacob. "She's up the hall. I saw her when you were getting cleaned up. Her ankle is bandaged and she's hooked up to the same bells and whistles you're hooked to. Unlike you, though, she probably won't have to spend the night." The docs had already told him that, given his medical history, he'd be a visitor at least until morning.

Surely Ivy wouldn't leave without seeing him, unless she saw no future for them.

But he had her affection. Right?

The nurse finished then stepped back. "All set. Do you need anything else, Special Agent Garcia?"

He really wanted to say "just Ivy," but one glance at Linc stopped that. "I'm fine. Thanks."

With a smile at him and an even bigger one at Linc, she left the room, pulling the door shut behind her.

Women always smiled at Linc. He rarely seemed to notice.

As soon as the door closed, he stepped farther in and

settled onto the chair by Jacob's bed. "Your sister's worried about you."

"Where is she, anyway?" Still wiped out from the ordeal, Jacob gingerly lifted his legs and settled on the propped-up bed.

"She's with Ivy. They let Angie bring Wren up."

Now he wanted to find Ivy even more than he had before. If Wren was in the building, he wanted both of them by his side. His family.

"Settle down, Sparky." Linc waved him back. "I've got questions as your team leader. Consider it an informal debrief."

Oh, yeah. He had a job. And he'd witnessed the demise of the most wanted criminal in the park. As fast as he could, he gave Linc a rundown of the encounter with Daniel Adams.

When he was finished, Linc nodded. "We have a team recovering the body. I turned your cell phone over to Agent Peterson at the FBI, as you requested. We should hear from him soon." Linc sat forward and clasped his hands between his knees. "That phone is how we found you."

He was kidding, right? "How? I busted it in the fire."

"It must have been the screen and not the guts. Highway patrol found the ambulance a couple of hours after you disappeared, but the slide had already wiped out the trail, so they assumed you didn't head down. Rescuers were searching toward the ranch until your phone pinged around seven this morning not far from the crash site. It briefly picked up a tower when you moved to that higher elevation. McCormick was able to track it for a couple of minutes, heading back down into the canyon, but lost it again. We had people on foot and sent the help up after a second ping around lunchtime."

They'd reached an elevated open area around that time before dipping down to the stream. How his broken cell phone had managed to have battery and signal strength at that point was beyond him. It had, and that was all that mattered. Well, that and... "Did they pick up Sienna Davies?"

Linc's grin made a reappearance. "When you told the rescue team she was out there, they got our team moving immediately. They picked her up on ATVs at the head of a ravine with two others. She's been tight-lipped, but they found the file in her vehicle at the trailhead with evidence pointing to Ross Evans's involvement with organized crime. The FBI should have him in custody as we speak."

So it was over. Ivy was officially safe.

He wasn't waiting any longer. "Let's go." Even though his entire body ached from the kind of pain that meds couldn't touch, he was going to find Ivy and Wren. He raised the bed higher and turned. "Get me unhooked from this—"

"And risk getting yelled at by that nurse? Nope." Linc stood. "I'll go see if she'll come back and—"

Two taps and the door eased open before Linc could touch it. Likely "that nurse" had sensed he was on the move.

Perfect. "Nurse, can you help me get these wires unhooked?"

"I don't think I'm qualified to do that." Ivy peeked around the door, her dark hair damp from a shower and her color much improved beneath the pink of sunburn on her face.

She'd never looked better.

Jacob exhaled the last of the tension from his body. She was safe. He was safe. They'd battled nature and more killers than he wanted to count…and they'd won. He sniffed away the emotion that tried to rise up in his chest. "You look…amazing."

Linc clicked his tongue and slipped past Ivy, throwing up a hand as he left. "And with that, I'm out."

Grinning, Ivy turned to watch him go. "Guess he's not very sentimental."

"It's why he's not married." He smiled to take away the sting of the comment. Linc was a confirmed bachelor. Marriage had never been on his radar. According to him it never would be.

But it was definitely on Jacob's. He crooked his index finger and beckoned Ivy forward. "Come here." She was killing him, standing so near but not beside him. He was done with worrying about her fears. Done with living life without her. While there would be some working through their past and the separation from Wren, he was done with wondering if he could forgive her.

Ivy hobbled in with a crutch under one arm, favoring her bandaged ankle. After closing the door, she leaned back against it. "Jacob." Her smile faded. She stared at the window across the room. Whatever was on her mind, it was heavy.

His chest caved in. If she tried to say goodbye to him after all they'd walked through together, he'd never—

"I'm sorry." She pressed her lips together as the first tear escaped and trailed down her cheek. "I'm sorry about Wren. I'm sorry I made those decisions about your life for you. Decisions about all of our lives. And I'm sorry I—"

"Ivy."

She held up her hand to stop his interruption. "I realized that I've kept Wren in this safe little box. And I've kept me in this safe little box. The bad things still found us. I stared down a killer's gun. I'm not a soldier or a police officer or a special agent, but I still stared down a gun, was shot at, had men try to choke the life from me... In life, I guess danger isn't particular to any job. And it's about trusting God, no matter what." She kept talking without taking a breath. "So I'm sorry I let you walk away the first time. That I didn't fight for us. That I was too scared to tell you I wanted to live my life with you and...I can't...do...that...again." She lifted her gaze to meet his. "I love you."

Those pleading brown eyes, the ones he'd dreamed of for over five years, pretty much undid the last of his reserves about what had happened between them.

His heart thumped faster and felt like it was beating for the first time since she walked away from him at UNLV.

Yeah, he had definitely forgiven her.

The monitor beside him had to be betraying him. When Ivy's gaze shifted and focused on it, he had no doubt the rapid rise and fall of his return to life were on that screen for all to see.

Carefully, he shifted his position so he sat on the edge of the bed. "Come here." He'd said it once already. Maybe this time, she'd move.

She sniffed and swiped her hands down her cheeks, smearing the tears that ran there. "I told Wren. She's, um..." She laughed gently. "She's wildly excited that *Jaycup* is her daddy. Angie has her now, trying to keep her occupied while we talk."

Now the tears pricked his eyes. She was breaking him

in the best of ways, handing him everything he'd ever wanted.

Except one. "Come *here*."

"She wants you to teach her to ride a horse."

"Ivy."

Her head swiveled back and forth. She had more to say. "Jacob, can you forgive—"

She didn't have to ask. "Ivy. Janelle. Bridges. *Come. Here.*"

With another sniff she finally pushed away from the door and approached slowly, relying on the crutch heavily, almost as though she expected him to change his mind. When she was only a few feet away, he leaned forward, grabbed her hand and helped her the rest of the way to him.

Looking up at her, he let his gaze wander her face, searching her eyes. They were alight with freedom. She'd finally released her fears.

Without taking his gaze from hers, he stood. The last time he'd been in a hospital bed, all he'd wanted was her.

And now, here she was.

He could fly if he really wanted to.

She inhaled a shaky breath. "Can you forgive me?" The whisper was low, quiet. She needed his affirmation.

Not trusting his voice, he nodded. *Oh, Ivy...*

Her eyes slipped closed and then her head was on his chest. She was trying not to hurt his arm in the sling between them.

But he wanted her closer. He planted his hand at the small of her back and drew her close. "Ivy?"

"What?" Her voice muffled against his chest.

"You said earlier today that you wanted a toothbrush more than anything in the world."

She laughed suddenly and nodded.

"Did you get one?"

She nodded again.

"Ivy?"

"What?" He could hear the smile in her voice. It seemed she knew where he was headed.

Jacob ran his hand up her back to her neck, then let his fingers trail along her jaw to her chin. He tilted her head up and brushed his lips against hers, hesitating with her breath on his. "I love you, too."

She didn't speak. Just reached up and pulled his head the rest of the way to her, kissing in a way that released all of her fears and promised him forever.

There was a click and a bang as the door flew open and bounced off the wall. "Jaycup!"

He pulled away from Ivy just as a force rocketed into his legs and nearly toppled them.

Wren wrapped hear arms around his legs and looked up at him. "Mama says if you say yes, we can all stay at your cabin forever."

He glanced at Ivy, who was wearing a sheepish grin. He disentangled himself from her embrace and sank to the edge of the bed, leaning forward to Wren's eye level. "If I say yes to what?"

"I don't know. But you're my daddy."

Coming from her mouth, the word was a sledgehammer to the chest, breaking through any remaining stone around his heart. "I am."

She patted his cheek. "I'm glad."

"Me, too." Pulling her close, he rested his chin on her head and found Ivy's eyes. They were leaking tears again, and they pulled a few from him as well. "So, how about, Wren, if *you* say yes, we can all live at my cabin."

"Yes to what?" She snuggled closer against him as though she'd always known who he was.

"Will you let me marry Mama?" He spoke without breaking Ivy's gaze.

As Wren shrieked her *yes* directly into his ear, Ivy wrapped her arms around both of them.

And Jacob was finally whole again.

* * * * *

If you enjoyed this story, look for these other books by Jodie Bailey:

Captured at Christmas
Under Surveillance

Dear Reader,

I'm so excited you joined Ivy and Jacob on their winding journey back to one another! You know, there were a lot of ways that Jacob's relationship with Ivy could have gone after he learned about Wren, but I really wanted him to show her grace. While he had to acknowledge that it would be easy, but I wanted him to have a love for her that was so big it overcame every obstacle between them. And Ivy needed to blossom under that kind of love, to see that fear has no place in love. I've known love that involved fear—of being abandoned, of being betrayed and of being emotionally hurt. The fears didn't come to fruition, but they kept me from loving with my whole heart. There was always that secret spot I kept guarded. That's no way to live. Love *without* fear is love *with* freedom. It's the kind of love God loves us with and that He wants us to love Him with in return!

Just so you know, I took a couple of liberties with the Grand Canyon and also with Jacob's investigative position for the sake of telling their story, because I wanted him to have that "battle buddy" in Linc, someone who'd known him for a while and would call him on his mistakes. May we all have a friend like that!

I hope you enjoyed Ivy and Jacob's story…and Wren's, too. And I hope you saw Jesus among the pages. I'd love to hear from you! You can drop by www.jodiebailey.com and find all sorts of ways to keep in touch!

Jodie Bailey

Get 4 FREE REWARDS!

We'll send you 2 FREE Books plus 2 FREE Mystery Gifts.

Both the **Love Inspired**® and **Love Inspired**® **Suspense** series feature compelling novels filled with inspirational romance, faith, forgiveness, and hope.

YES! Please send me 2 FREE novels from the Love Inspired or Love Inspired Suspense series and my 2 FREE gifts (gifts are worth about $10 retail). After receiving them, if I don't wish to receive any more books, I can return the shipping statement marked "cancel." If I don't cancel, I will receive 6 brand-new Love Inspired or Love Inspired Suspense Larger-Print books every month and be billed just $5.99 each in the U.S. or $6.24 each in Canada. That is a savings of at least 17% off the cover price. It's quite a bargain! Shipping and handling is just 50¢ per book in the U.S. and $1.25 per book in Canada.* I understand that accepting the 2 free books and gifts places me under no obligation to buy anything. I can always return a shipment and cancel at any time. The free books and gifts are mine to keep no matter what I decide.

Choose one: ☐ **Love Inspired**
Larger-Print
(122/322 IDN GNWC)

☐ **Love Inspired Suspense**
Larger-Print
(107/307 IDN GNWN)

Name (please print)

Address   Apt. #

City   State/Province   Zip/Postal Code

Email: Please check this box ☐ if you would like to receive newsletters and promotional emails from Harlequin Enterprises ULC and its affiliates. You can unsubscribe anytime.

Mail to the Harlequin Reader Service:
IN U.S.A.: P.O. Box 1341, Buffalo, NY 14240-8531
IN CANADA: P.O. Box 603, Fort Erie, Ontario L2A 5X3

Want to try 2 free books from another series? Call 1-800-873-8635 or visit www.ReaderService.com.

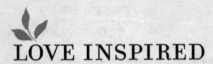